SECRETS OF THE BELMONT LODGE

SECRETS OF THE BELMONT LODGE

First edition. December 31, 2024.

Copyright © 2024 K. D. Jackson.

ISBN: 979-8227919830

Written by K. D. Jackson.

Table of Contents

For my sister, *Kerah*.

Thank you for teaching me to never underestimate a powerful deaf woman.

PROLOGUE

Aspen, Colorado – 1893

The Belmont family lodge was alive with the festive spirit of winter. Snow had fallen steadily throughout the day, blanketing the landscape in a thick, white silence. An eeriness hung heavy in the air. Inside, the grand ballroom glittered with the reflections of a thousand lights from the ornate crystal chandeliers. It would surprise anyone to know the value of the intricate decor. Laughter and music filled the air as guests danced and mingled, unaware of the dark secrets that lurked beneath the lodge's spectacular facade.

In the dimly lit servant's quarters, a young maid named Lily sat alone, her heart heavy with a secret. She clutched a worn, leather-bound diary. Her fingers traced the words she had penned just hours before. The diary was her confidante, a silent witness to the forbidden love affair she had embarked upon with William Belmont, the middle son of the illustrious family.

Lily's love for William was a dangerous transgression, a spark of passion that threatened to ignite a powder keg of scandal and betrayal. She knew the risks and potential consequences of their clandestine meetings and stolen kisses. But her young and naive heart had been captivated by William's charm, charisma, and promises of a love that transcended the rigid social hierarchy of the lodge.

As she reread the diary entries, a shiver ran down her spine. She had written of stolen moments in hidden alcoves, whispered conversations in moonlit gardens, and a love that defied the conventions of their world. But she had also hinted at a growing unease, a sense of foreboding that their secret could not remain hidden forever.

The lodge, with its labyrinth of corridors and hidden passages, was a place of secrets, a silent witness to the passions and betrayals that unfolded within its walls. Lily had always felt a strange connection to the lodge as if its very stones whispered of the forgotten loves and tragic endings. She tried to ignore the pull of the voices telling her that her own story may also soon fill the halls. That she, too, may become a secret of the past.

She had heard the rumors, the whispers of ghostly apparitions and unexplained occurrences. The staff spoke in hushed tones of the former maid, Mary, who had disappeared decades ago without a trace, her fate shrouded in mystery. Some said she had been murdered, her body hidden somewhere within the lodge's vast expanse. Others claimed she had simply run away, unable to bear the weight of the lodge's secrets; neither idea was too inconceivable.

Lily had always dismissed these stories as mere superstition, the idle gossip of bored servants. But now, as she sat alone in her room with the diary clutched tightly in her hand, she couldn't shake the feeling that there was more to the lodge's history than met the eye.

A sudden creak of the floorboards startled Lily awake. She looked up, feeling an intense beating in her chest. A visitor at that hour could never be good. The door to her room stood ajar, a sliver of light cutting through the darkness. A figure emerged from the shadows, their face obscured by the dim light.

Lily's breath caught in her throat. She recognized the tall, imposing form of Charles Belmont, the eldest son. His face was a mask of cold fury. A palpable wave of hate and unease seemed to envelop the space around him.

"Lily," Charles said, his voice a menacing whisper that sent more chills down her spine, "we need to talk."

Lily's heart sank. She knew what this meant. Her secret was out. The consequences of her forbidden love were about to unfold, and she was powerless to stop them.

Charles stepped into the room with his eyes fixed on Lily's trembling form. He held a small, leather-bound book in his hand, its cover worn and faded. Lily recognized it instantly with its dark cover and the purple heart she had drawn on the front. It was her diary, the repository of her deepest secrets and her most intimate thoughts. Over and over and over, Lily wondered how he had gotten ahold of her diary. She thought she remembered falling asleep with it.

"I found this," Charles said, his voice dripping with contempt. "It seems you have been keeping secrets from us, dear."

Lily's face paled. Her eyes widened with terror. She tried to speak, but the words caught in her throat. All that escaped was a faint whimper and a shudder.

Charles opened the diary, his eyes scanning the pages with a predatory intensity. He read aloud excerpts of her entries, his voice dripping with sarcasm and disgust. He mocked her naive declarations of love, her foolish dreams of a future with William. Charles gave a hint of amusement at Lily's unsettled presence.

Lily, humiliated, could only stand there, her body trembling with barely suppressed sobs. She had been exposed, her vulnerability laid bare for all to see.

Charles closed the diary with a snap. His eyes burned into hers, and they stung more than the tears Lily was fighting. "You have betrayed our trust, Lily," he said, his voice cold and unforgiving. "You have disgraced my family."

Lily, her voice barely a whisper, tried to defend herself, "I love him," she said. Her eyes pleaded for understanding. "We didn't mean to hurt anyone."

Charles scoffed, and his lip curled in disgust. "Love?" he spat. "You call that love? It's nothing but a childish infatuation, a fleeting fancy that will pass with time. You are just a maid. You are absolutely nothing. William could never love you."

He stepped closer, his voice dropping to a hiss, "But your actions have consequences, Lily. You have crossed a line, and you will pay the price."

Lily's heart pounded against her ribs, and her mind raced with fear. She knew that she was in danger; Charles would do anything to protect his family's reputation.

"Please," she begged, her voice trembling, "don't hurt me."

Charles's eyes narrowed, his expression hardening. "You have already hurt us," he said. "It's only appropriate that we do the same."

With a swift movement, Charles grabbed Lily's arm with a vice-like grip. The thick walls of the lodge muffled her cries of pain. The corridors were nothing but a maze to isolate the helpless.

Charles dragged her towards the door, his face a stone of chilling rage. Lily struggled to break free, but his grasp was too strong. She was being taken to a place of darkness, a place where secrets were buried and lives were extinguished. Lily did not doubt that Mary's disappearance was not of her own doing. Lily was simply too afraid to accept the other girl's fate—afraid it may become her own. Her spirit may become the lies of a maid named Lily who ran away.

The shadows that danced in the firelight seemed to mock her, their whispers a constant reminder of the danger that lurked just beyond the door. Lily should have listened to her unease. Mary had met the same fate as Lily.

As Charles dragged her through the darkened corridors, Lily's heart pounded with despair. She knew that her fate was sealed; her love for William had led her to this moment of reckoning. Lily's mother had told her when she was young that great love was worth everything—even death. She held onto these words in her final moments.

Charles drew a pistol from its holster while Lily collapsed to her knees. The lodge's secrets stretched deeper and deeper, and she had to pay the ultimate price. Lily was a pawn in a game of power and betrayal. The sort of darkness that had always lurked beneath the surface of the lodge was about to consume her, and there was nothing she could do to stop it.

CHAPTER ONE—Arrival

Aspen, Colorado – 2024

Staring out the window at the falling snow, Emily Parker felt a mix of anticipation and anxiety. The snow-capped peaks of Mount Riviera loomed in the distance, both majestic and imposing. She looked over at Scott, who was driving cautiously on the icy road. She asked, "How do you feel about seeing everyone?"

With one hand steady on the wheel, Scott's fingers moving smoothly through the signs, his grin spreading across his face. "Honestly, I'm not sure how to feel." The passing streetlights cast alternating shadows across his face as he stole a glance at her. His smile softened, growing more genuine. "I'm sure it will be memorable." He returned his attention to the road stretching before them, but the warmth in his expression lingered.

Emily smiled. Scott had been her best friend for as long as she could remember. He had picked up a significant amount of sign language over the years, and while he wasn't fluent, he could understand and communicate with Emily just fine.

Emily primarily communicated through ASL, but she often whispered along with her signs—a habit she'd developed to help friends like Scott who were still learning. While she could read lips well enough, signing remained most natural for her, with her soft voice serving as a gentle bridge between both worlds.

It had been ten years since they all graduated from Glenwood High School, and their dear friend Claire Wilson had planned this entire weekend trip. She had always been a planner and had helped hold the friend group together. Claire was a straight edge, but she was very sweet.

A few years ago, Claire had married David Belmont. He was extremely wealthy, and in turn, Claire was wealthy as well. David owned several properties across the United States, but he and Claire swore nothing beat the view from the historic lodge in Aspen.

David was not just a successful businessman; he was a man of many layers. Though his name was practically royalty, he had grown up in the shadow of faded wealth. The Belmonts had thrived for generations, but after decades of extravagance, the family fortune had dwindled to almost nothing. David had worked tirelessly to restore both the family's wealth and their ancestral lodge to their former glory. David had to rebuild his family name and provide for himself.

Emily had never visited Colorado apart from a connecting flight. To actually experience the state was magical. She felt so small surrounded by the towering mountains, all covered in white snow. She really hadn't ventured far from their small hometown, so the vastness was almost overwhelming. The pristine beauty of the landscape was surreal, like stepping into a postcard.

Emily looked back at her *chauffeur*. She and Scott had been inseparable since grade school. Very few people in the school knew sign language, and it was difficult for Emily to make friends. No one tried except for Scott. Their bond was special. To be honest, she always suspected he had feelings for her, but he never asked her out. Sometimes she wondered what it would be like if Scott did ask her out. Her life would completely change.

As they drove, her mind wandered to Mark Evans, who she heard would be attending the lodge reunion. Emily wasn't entirely pleased that he would be there, mostly because she didn't want to face him so many years later. They dated all four years at Glenwood High, but their relationship had ended messily. He also happened to be Claire's fraternal twin, so it made escaping him that much harder.

Emily never wanted to break up the friend group, but she just didn't trust Mark anymore. His betrayal had cut deep, leaving Emily feeling worthless and unwanted. She had retreated into the world of books, seeking solace in their pages and avoiding the painful reminders of her shattered dreams. The pain had been so intense, so all-consuming, that she had vowed never to let herself be that vulnerable again.

Mark was always getting into fights, showing up to school with a black eye and busted lip. She knew he was trouble. The rest of her friends saw him as an immature, funny boy who treated his problems flippantly.

Emily knew there was something deeper, but she tried to ignore it for the sake of their relationship. After trusting her gut, she caught him cheating on her and broke things off immediately, refusing any excuses from Mark. The last time she saw him was at their graduation. He quietly left the ceremony in the passenger seat of Claire's car. That was ten years ago, and she hadn't anticipated seeing him ever again.

"Hey, are you alright?" The question hung between them, and from the patient set of his shoulders, she realized he must have asked more than once.

"Come back," he laughed softly, his expression a familiar vigilance. It was that same observant nature that had made him such a natural fit for law enforcement after graduation. Even now, off-duty, his police training showed in the way he read people, picking up on subtle shifts in mood and expression with an ease that still surprised her.

Emily blinked, snapping back to the present. "Yeah, just thinking about old times. Crazy we're about to see them. It's been a long while."

Scott reached over and squeezed her hand. "Don't worry, Ems. Once the fun starts, the weekend will be over before you know it." He paused, adding with a joking wink, "And you know, if it's as chaotic as we expect it to be, we can fake an emergency and skip town first thing tomorrow morning."

Emily covered her mouth to conceal a laugh. "Honestly, we may have to do just that."

"Yeah? Maybe we don't even stay the night," Scott said. "Why don't we stop by, say hello and turn right back around?"

"We don't even have to go at all," Emily smacked his arm. "Let's turn around right now!"

Scott pretended to turn the steering wheel, and they both dissolved into laughter.

Emily smiled, grateful for his unwavering support. Scott had always been there for her through thick and thin. He was her rock, her confidant, and the one person she could always count on. Why had he never asked her out?

Emily shook the thought away and focused on the majestic scenery. She got a glimpse of her reflection in the window, making eye contact with the green eyes and light brown hair staring back at her. The mountains were in the distance, forming soft lines between the freckles of her reflection.

The drive to Belmont Lodge was nothing short of a winter wonderland adventure. Towering pine trees, their branches overloaded with snow, flanked the narrow, winding roads. Emily's breath fogged up the truck window while she marveled at the serene beauty outside. The mountains stood in the distance, their peaks kissed by the early morning sun.

Scott, ever the careful driver, navigated the icy roads with a calm precision that Emily found comforting. As they climbed higher into the mountains, the air grew colder and crisper, filling the car with the invigorating scent of pine and fresh snow.

When they approached the lodge, Emily's anxiety began to rise again. She hadn't seen most of these people in years, and she wasn't sure how they would react to her. She wondered if they would still see her as the shy, nerdy girl she had been in high school or if they would recognize the confident and successful woman she had become. Emily felt she had changed quite a bit since school, and she hoped it was noticeable.

Scott, sensing her unease, reached over and squeezed her hand again. "Over before you know it."

She smiled, feeling a flutter in her stomach. The navigation read 20 minutes until the lodge, and Emily decided to treat her anxieties as excitement.

"Is it a little warm?" she asked, scooting to the side of her seat.

"Ah, sorry, seat warmer," Scott answered, turning off the setting. "I just thought—surrounded by all this snow..."

Emily repositioned herself, unable to help the blush that crept into her cheeks at his unwavering little acts of chivalry.

When Scott's truck pulled into the lodge's driveway, the two of them were taken aback by its extravagance. This was not an everyday log cabin; it could easily be mistaken for a Hilton Hotel. The lodge was nestled amongst a grove of towering trees. Dark wood covered the exterior of the lodge. Large windows offered glimpses inside.

The place seemed to sparkle in the sun. Emily was so mesmerized, she momentarily forgot that she was allowed to go inside. It seemed too beautiful for her to be granted access.

When they exited the vehicle, a woman approached, introduced herself, and offered to take their luggage. Her thick accent sounded Polish. She was small with curly dark red hair.

"Welcome, I am Meredith. I'll take your bags. Let's go inside now, dears." Her voice was chipper, proper, and yet reserved. She didn't sign to them, but Emily could read her lips just fine; she spoke with a swift clearness.

"Thank you, ma'am," Scott said, clearing his throat.

Meredith responded with a small nod.

Emily and Scott exchanged a surprised glance. They hadn't been expecting a personal assistant to greet them at the door. Meredith, with her neatly pressed uniform and efficient manner, seemed out of place in the rustic setting.

The pair followed Meredith up the front steps, their boots crunching in the fresh snow. The air was crisp, and Emily could see her breath forming clouds in front of her face.

The large front doors opened before them, and Claire was waiting in the doorway. Her face beamed with excitement as she bounced with joy. "Emily! Scott! Look at you two, still so close! Welcome to the Belmont family lodge!"

Claire, the mastermind behind the reunion, had kept everyone connected. It was the first time they had all been together since high school.

"Claire, it has really been too long," Emily wrapped her in a hug, her ears already stinging from the cold mountain air.

"Please, come in, come in!" Claire ushered them inside, closing the front doors behind them.

"Beautiful place, Claire, really," Scott said.

Emily and Scott stepped inside to escape the cold. Immediately, Emily marveled at the extravagance. Winding staircases reached the ceilings, and chandeliers twinkled in the firelight. Photos of past lives and happy reunions filled the walls.

"You guys, this is my husband, David!" Claire said, beaming.

She gestured to her husband. He stood in the lobby in front of the grand fireplace. He appeared even wealthier in person than he did on Facebook. David was tall and lean, with salt-and-pepper hair and a warm smile. He exuded an air of confidence and success, but there was also a hint of grief in his eyes that Emily couldn't quite place. Emily had always been good at reading facial clues. Words were only half the story.

David's eyes, often kind, held a shadow of regret and the burden of secrets. His relationship with Claire, while appearing perfect, had its complexities. Emily sensed a certain distance between them, a subtle tension that made her wonder what lay beneath the polished exterior of their marriage.

"It's a pleasure to finally meet you, David," Scott said with a firm handshake.

"Pleasure's all mine. It's nice to put a face to all the names! Oh, uh—Emily, Claire taught me some sign language! Let me try ..." David fumbled his fingers for a minute and signed, "Hi, my name is B-A-F-I-B."

Emily watched silently for a moment before breaking the tension. She was used to people showing off their sign language skills to her and often had to hold back laughter while they failed tremendously. "That was ... very good!" Emily replied. "You know, it's the effort that counts." They all laughed, the ice breaking slightly. Warmth filled the room, a nice welcome to the weekend.

"Meredith honey, can you bring the bags to their rooms?" Claire ordered.

"Of course," Meredith responded in a calm tone.

David turned to Emily. "You read lips?"

"Yes," Emily smiled.

"Okay, thank goodness," David wiped his forehead. "I do not know hardly any sign language."

"I'll let it slide this one time," Emily teased, "but next time I see you—you better be fluent."

Claire stepped in toward the group, her body language warm and inviting. "You guys don't have to stay by the doors, please, explore and make yourselves at home!"

"The lodge was built sometime in the early 1800s," David explained. "Survived some terrible storms, but we did some serious demo work and the bones are still there."

"It's breathtaking, man," Scott chimed in.

"We'll be right down here if you need anything at all," Claire said. "Excuse us for just one moment."

As the two of them stepped toward the kitchen, Emily and Scott began to explore.

While they walked around, they were enchanted by each of the paintings and vintage light fixtures that decorated every wall in the hallway. The lodge was a masterpiece of rustic elegance with exposed wooden beams, stone fireplaces, and plush furnishings. The walls were adorned with artwork that ranged from classic landscapes to modern abstracts. Thick, hand-woven rugs covered the floors. They could explore the halls for weeks and still find new secrets every day.

Emily couldn't help but feel a sense of awe as she took in her surroundings. She had never been in a place like this before, and she began wondering what it would be like to live in such luxury. The lodge seemed to be a perfect sanctuary from the outside world.

The main hallway stretched before them, its hardwood floors gleaming under antique light fixtures. Afternoon sunlight filtered through tall windows, casting long shadows across Persian rugs. Emily's boots sank into the plush carpeting as they walked.

"Look at the detail in everything," Emily signed, running her fingers along the dark wood paneling. The surface was smooth, expertly refinished.The lodge's original charm was preserved while incorporating elements of contemporary architecture. Brass light fixtures had been polished to a warm glow.

They passed a series of family portraits—generations of Belmonts staring down with stern expressions. Emily paused at one showing a woman in a high-necked Victorian dress, her hair pulled severely back. "The details in these are incredible," she signed. "Look at the brushwork on her dress."

Scott leaned closer to examine the painting. "Hard to believe some of these are over a hundred years old." He squinted at the small brass plaque beneath. "Elizabeth Belmont, 1892."

They continued down the hall, discovering a music room that opened through a wide archway. A grand piano dominated the space, its black surface reflecting the wall sconces like stars. Sheet music had been left open on the stand—something by Chopin, the pages yellow with age.

"Claire mentioned David's been gradually furnishing each room," Emily signed, moving to examine a collection of leather-bound books on nearby shelves. Their spines were cracked with age, titles faded to near illegibility.

Scott wandered to the windows, where heavy velvet curtains framed a view of the surrounding forest. Snow had begun falling again, fat flakes drifting past the glass. "The isolation up here is something else," he signed. "Can't even see the main road anymore."

Emily joined him at the window. The snow-covered grounds stretched toward dense pine forest, branches heavy with white. The silence felt absolute—even the usual vibrations she sensed through the floorboards seemed muted by the snow.

They discovered a conservatory next, its glass ceiling soaring three stories up. Dead leaves from past seasons crunched under their feet. Terra cotta pots sat empty on wrought iron stands, waiting for spring planting. The space smelled of earth and dormant things.

"This would be beautiful in summer," Emily signed, imagining the room filled with greenery and light.

Scott nodded. "Maybe Claire will let us come back when it's warm." He paused, then added with a grin, "Though I bet the heating bill for this room alone is insane."

They found the kitchen next, a vast space with modern appliances alongside original features. A massive hearth dominated one wall, its cooking crane still intact. Copper pots hung from ceiling racks, and the center island could have seated twelve comfortably.

"No wonder Meredith likes working here," Emily signed. "This kitchen is a dream."

Scott opened one of the pantry doors, revealing shelves stocked with enough food for weeks. "David and Claire really planned for this reunion," he signed. "Look at all this."

Emily was examining a set of antique cookie molds hanging on the wall when she felt vibrations through the floor—footsteps approaching. Claire appeared in the doorway, looking pleased to find them.

"Getting the grand tour?" she asked, her smile warm. "I got lost three times my first time here. The layout takes some getting used to."

"It's incredible," Emily signed. "The restoration work is amazing."

Claire beamed with pride. "David's put his heart into this place. Come on, I'll show you the dining room. We should start thinking about dinner anyway—everyone will be arriving soon."

As they followed Claire, Emily glanced back at the kitchen. Sunset had painted the copper pots deep red, their surfaces reflecting the light like dying embers.

Just as they returned to the foyer, another familiar face was conversing with Claire and David. Alice Thompson, who had not aged a single day since senior year, spotted them with a smile. Alice was the petite and bubbly girl who had always been the life of the party. She was head cheerleader in high school, and she maintained that same peppiness even to this day. Emily had always admired her infectious energy and positive outlook on life. Alice had a way of making everyone around her feel special, and Emily had been looking forward to seeing her again.

"Ems?" Alice shouted while sprinting toward them. Emily wrapped Alice in a hug, noting how tiny she still was even in heels. She was small, but the force of the hug still almost took Emily to the ground. Alice's blonde hair was nearly to her waist, and her cheeks were pink and full of life. She smiled up at Emily.

"It doesn't feel real seeing you. You haven't aged a day since high school," Emily signed.

Alice replied, "Shut up. I look so different! Girl, this place is so nice, huh? I've been walking around and trying not to get lost even though I've been here a couple of times. Claire and David let me come a couple of days early, so I've been getting comfy. Did you meet Meredith? She's the best, so sweet. Do you want to see your room?" It was rare for Alice to take a breath, her words running a hundred miles an hour.

"Of course! Give me the grand tour, Ali," Emily said, grinning from ear to ear in the company of her dear friend. They walked up the stairs, but it felt as though they were hiking. Every vast hallway looked the same, with Meredith dusting the paintings and flower vases on every little side table.

"So, tell me about New York?" Emily asked.

"It's not even that crazy, a lot of people live in New York, Ems."

"At least you left Utah!" Emily exclaimed. "I mean, I love it of course, but it's not New York City!"

Alice rolled her eyes, still smiling. "Whatever."

"So," Alice said suddenly, "are you going to tell me if you're sleeping with *Officer Scott Simmons*, or should I keep my assumptions to myself?"

Emily quietly gasped. "God, Alice! No, we are definitely not sleeping together. We're only friends, nothing more." Emily chuckled." Scott is a very ... interesting person. I mean, he's sweet, and we hang out all the time. The sheriff's station is right across the street from my library, and sometimes he'll come by in the morning to bring me these little scones," she blushed. "I think we just work well as close, close friends." Emily didn't know whether to keep laughing or to be embarrassed.

Alice rolled her eyes. "Mmhmm. *Friends*, for sure. Honey, I've known you since we were fourteen, and that's the most you've ever talked about a boy."

"He's- he's just-" Emily stammered. "It's rare that you find a gentleman nowadays, a real gentleman. I don't want to ruin what we have going on."

"Trust me, girl, I get it," Alice said. "But I was around you two for a total of ten seconds and the tension between you is unbelievable."

Emily laughed as they entered her suite. She shrugged the conversation off and focused on the vastness of the space before her, grateful for the escape.

The bedroom was bigger than her entire apartment back in Glenwood. A king-size bed and a royal plush rug stretched nearly wall to wall. Blackout curtains covered an enormous window with the most spectacular view of Mount Riviera. There was even a laundry chute next to the walk-in closet. Emily was in complete awe.

Alice squealed, "Insane? I know. Mine is right next door. Let's go back downstairs. I want you to finally meet Brian!" Alice, squirming with excitement, leaped out of the door toward the stairs they had just so recently trekked. Emily wasn't very athletic, so she expected these steps to be the death of her by the end of the weekend. It seemed that there were more stairs going down than there were going up.

Brian Hansen was Alice's boyfriend. Emily didn't know Brian as well as the others, but she had heard he was a talented photographer with a charming personality. She was curious to see how he fit in with the rest of the group.

Emily hoped Brian would be a good match for Alice, who deserved nothing but the best. Alice hadn't had the best of luck with guys treating her right in high school, so Emily felt protective. Alice always seemed drawn to the kinds of boys who would take advantage of her.

Emily had already begun to have a change of heart for this vacation. Maybe it wouldn't be *that* bad. She was mostly nervous about her inevitable encounter with Mark and seeing everyone again, but she knew she could at least count on Scott, Claire, and Alice to help her have a good time.

They walked down the final stairway and into the living room where the rest of the group had gathered. It seemed Mark had arrived since Emily and Alice had been upstairs. He had grown out his dark hair nearly to his shoulders, and it complemented his new facial hair. She nodded in his direction.

Alice wrapped Brian in a hug as if she hadn't just seen him a few minutes ago. Emily wondered what it must be like to love someone like that. Alongside Claire, Alice had also been key in holding their group together. Her cackling laughter and persistent optimism were a beacon of light, even during their darkest days in high school.

Alice's journey after graduation had taken her far from their hometown, but her spirit remained unchanged. She had faced her own set of challenges, including a tumultuous relationship that ended in heartbreak. Meeting Brian was a turning point for her.

Brian and Emily quickly introduced themselves. He held Alice around the waist. "How was the drive up here?" he asked.

Emily smirked. "Not too bad."

Brian placed his hand on Alice's cheek as he prepared a kiss. Emily was happy for Alice, and hoped she had finally found someone who treasured her.

The living room was serene and inviting. A flame roared in the fireplace so tall Emily could stand in it, and plush sofas were arranged in a semicircle. The group had settled in, drinks in hand, and they began to catch up.

Seeing everyone together warmed Emily's heart as much as the flames. Emily poured herself a glass of some very expensive-looking whiskey. Judging by how much everyone else had in their glasses, Emily thought perhaps she was not supposed to pour so much. Granted, she didn't usually drink dark liquor.

"Damn, Ems," Scott signed as Emily took a seat next to him. "Save any for the rest of us?"

Emily chuckled, took a sip, and very quickly became aware of why she was only supposed to have a little bit.

Mark Evans sat by the fireplace looking contemplative. When Emily and Alice entered, he looked up and offered a small, somewhat strained smile. He hadn't changed much. He was still ruggedly handsome but with an air of brooding intensity.

As Emily sipped her whiskey, she couldn't help but feel a swirl of emotions. It was surreal to see everyone after so many years, and though the initial welcome was exciting, she couldn't shake off the unease that had settled in her chest.

High school had been a mixed bag of memories for her with moments of happiness overshadowed by betrayal and misunderstandings. She wondered how much everyone had changed and whether they would accept her for the person she had become.

The thought of interacting with Mark again after all these years was particularly daunting. Their breakup had been an unforgettable affair, and she wasn't sure if time had healed the wounds or simply buried them deeper. She wanted to give Mark a chance to show her the person he was now. She knew people changed and wanted to give him the benefit of the doubt.

Claire, ever the hostess, clinked her glass to get everyone's attention. Several people jerked their heads toward the sound, clearly lost in thought. "All right, everyone. I just want to say how amazing it is to have us all together again. It's been too long. Here's to old friends and new memories."

"Cheers!" the group echoed, raising their glasses.

"And to looking good and kicking ass," David declared. A few awkward chuckles spread through the group, and one "hell yeah!" came from Scott.

David took a seat next to Claire, his arm draped casually around her shoulders.

"So, does anyone remember that camping trip in junior year?" Mark asked, a mischievous glint in his eye.

Claire rolled her eyes at her brother's change in topic.

"The uh- the one in Raspert Park?" Scott asked.

"When your tent ripped and you woke up to the-" Emily began.

"Oh, don't remind me," Scott groaned. "I'm still traumatized from that encounter with the raccoon."

Alice smiled, remembering the chaos of the trip. "And the time we got lost trying to find the waterfall? We ended up hiking in circles for hours." She giggled. "I think that was the first time I realized we were not cut out for wilderness adventures."

Brian, Alice's boyfriend, chimed in. "Sounds like you guys had quite the adventure. I wish I could've been there."

"Oh, you would have loved it, Brian," Mark said. "It was a mess, but we had a lot of fun. And Scott's face when he ran from the raccoon—priceless."

The group laughed, the tension easing as they reminisced about their high school days. The conversation flowed naturally, each person contributing their favorite memories.

"I remember when Emily tutored me in Algebra," Alice said, smiling at Emily. "I was so hopeless, but you were so patient."

"Yeah, Emily was always the smart one," Claire added. "I wouldn't have passed chemistry without her help."

Scott added, "And she kept us all out of trouble. Well, most of the time." A small chuckle escaped his lips, remembering.

Emily felt an uncomfortable lump in her throat, touched by their words. She had always tried to be there for her friends, even when it wasn't easy. Despite everything, they had always been there for her too. Well, except Mark, but she didn't care. At least that's what she kept telling herself. Emily had always thought of Claire and Alice as the ones who held the group together, but maybe she should take some of the credit, too.

As the evening went on, the group continued to share stories and laugh together, the bonds of friendship growing stronger with each passing moment. Emily felt a sense of warmth and belonging that she hadn't felt in years. This reunion was exactly what she needed, and she was grateful to Claire for bringing them all together.

Eventually, the conversation turned to their plans for the weekend. Claire had arranged for a variety of activities, from skiing and snowboarding to spa treatments and gourmet dinners. There was something for everyone, and Emily was excited to see what the weekend escape would bring.

"Have you ever built an igloo?" Scott asked the group.

"I'm not an eskimo, Scott," Claire shook her head.

"Aw man, I would always do that with my brothers." Scott scratched his beard. "Brick by brick, the roof is the hardest part but once it's done it looks so cool."

"That sounds awesome," David interjected.

"How big are we talking?" Brian asked, smiling.

Claire looked at Emily and Alice. "Boys will be boys," she said, her eyes sarcastic.

Emily smiled along with her, but honestly, she thought building an igloo with them would be fun.

As they sat by the fire, basking in the glow of friendship and nostalgia, none of them could have predicted the dark turn their reunion would soon take.

Emily fell asleep on the couch, cradling a half-empty whiskey glass. Scott, ever the gentleman, carried her up the stairs and into her bed. He left a small peck on her forehead and whispered "goodnight" against her cheek before he closed the door. Even in her slight unconsciousness, a smile pricked at her lips, and warmth flowed through her.

As Emily lay sleeping, the sky darkened quickly, and the temperature dropped a few degrees in the lodge. An eerie vibration pulsated through the ground. Her eyelids fluttered open, and she stirred. However, the pull of slumber and whiskey was too strong, and she drifted back into the depths of sleep.

Minutes later, the vibration returned, stronger this time. Emily rolled over, her eyes still heavy with sleep. Her heart skipped a beat when she glimpsed a dark figure standing silently in the doorway. It simply watched her. The moment Emily's gaze landed on the figure, the door creaked shut. A chill ran down her spine as she sat up abruptly, sweat rolling down her forehead. She rushed out of bed and into the hallway, her eyes darting around in search of the intruder. There was no one there.

Emily's mind raced, trying to make sense of what she had just witnessed. Could she have imagined it? The fatigue and remnants of alcohol could have played tricks on her mind. She tried to convince herself that it was just a vivid dream. It wouldn't have been the first time.

Attempting to shake off the unsettling experience, Emily made her way back to her bedroom, her eyes glued to the floor, half-expecting to see footprints or any sign of the mysterious figure. But the floor was spotless.

When she lay down, Emily tried to dismiss the incident as a figment of her imagination. Deep down, she couldn't shake the feeling that something had been lurking in the shadows that night, watching her.

CHAPTER TWO—Snow

Friday

Claire woke the entire house at 6 a.m. with the clanging of pots and pans. This did not work for Emily, but Alice woke her by jumping into her bed. Emily swiped at Alice and groaned. She had never been much of a morning person.

"I'm up, I'm up," Emily grumbled, fighting a losing battle with her unruly bedhead. She caught her reflection in the window and winced.

"How did you sleep?" Alice's voice was far too cheerful for this hour.

"Good-ish?" Emily stifled a yawn. "Took forever to drift off, but once I did..." She shrugged, still working her fingers through tangled strands. "You?"

"Like I died and went to heaven!" She flopped backwards onto the bed, bouncing slightly. "These beds are absolutely criminal. I might have to steal it."

Emily laughed despite herself, knuckling sleep from her eyes. "Yeah, it definitely beats my lumpy futon back home."

"Meredith is downstairs working her breakfast magic." The smell of bacon wafted up, as if on cue. "We should probably make an appearance, babe."

"Just..." Emily waved vaguely at her entire disheveled state. "Give me five to transform into a human being. I'll meet you down there."

The rest of the group made their way downstairs, rubbing their eyes and stifling yawns. They were greeted by the smell of a wonderful breakfast Meredith had prepared: scrambled eggs, bacon, waffles, blueberry scones, and, best of all, coffee. Emily couldn't think straight without a cup of coffee, and the rich aroma brought her back to life almost as much as the actual kick of caffeine.

"Good morning, everyone." Claire beamed, her energy boundless. "I thought we could kick off the weekend with a morning ski outing. Mount Riviera is practically in our backyard."1

Mark, still waking up, managed a smile. "Sounds great, Claire. I need to wake up a bit first, though. I love you, but I kinda want to punch you right now. With love of course."

Scott, ever the supportive friend, chimed in. "I'm with Mark. A little caffeine boost before hitting the slopes sounds like a good plan."

Claire, undeterred by their initial grogginess, bustled around the kitchen, pouring coffee and offering plates of food. "Come on, guys, fuel up. It's going to be an amazing day."

As the group ate breakfast and Emily chugged two cups of coffee, the conversation slowly picked up. The group's bonding from the previous night seemed to have contributed to a sense of anticipation for the day ahead.

Suddenly, Emily had a fleeting memory of the night before when she woke to the figure in her room. Fully awake now, it seemed more like a dream and less like reality. The nervous energy stuck with Emily, but she decided not to think about it. It was just a dream, after all. That whiskey had been very strong.

"So, Emily," Alice said, her bright and cheerful voice pulling Emily out of her haze, "tell me about things in Glenwood. Is it the same as when we left?"

Emily smiled, grateful for the change of topic. "It is. I love that little town."

"That's so sweet," Alice replied. "Brian and I have been meaning to take a trip there. I can't wait to show him our old schools, childhood homes, and your library!"

Emily laughed. "You know you're always welcome to visit."

Mark, who had been listening quietly, spoke up. "Still reading all the time, huh?" He grinned. "You were always so smart."

A slight blush crept up Emily's cheeks. It felt like an honest compliment, yet it was strange to hear it from him. "Thanks, Mark. That's nice of you to say."

She glanced at Scott who was watching her with a warm smile. Scott placed a gentle hand on Emily's back, easing her stress.

After breakfast, the group dressed in their snow gear and met in the lobby. Emily had enjoyed a little skiing as a child, but it had been quite a few years since she last attempted it. Her stomach was a flurry of nervousness, excitement, and too much coffee as they bundled up and headed out into the morning mountain air.

The lodge was located by the base of Mount Riviera, a popular ski resort known for its challenging slopes and breathtaking views. The group loaded into two black SUVs—Claire and David in one, and the rest in the other, driven by Scott.

As they drove up the winding mountain road, Emily couldn't help but marvel at the scenery. She had seen it from a distance on the drive-in, but up close, it was even more dazzling. The snow-covered peaks glistened in the morning sun, and the air was so clear that she could see for miles despite the whisper of snow dusting the windshield.

Emily's phone cast a blue glow across her face as the alert flashed: *Severe Winter Storm Warning.* "Scott—"

He waved off her concern with an easy laugh. "Welcome to Colorado." His boots propped up on the coffee table, radiating local confidence. "Trust me, these storms roll through like clockwork. Weather folks always oversell it."

"Yeah," Mark drawled, leaning too far into her personal space. "You're in snowtown, honey."

Emily's shoulders stiffened. "I get it," she said, her tone clipped. The pet name from Mark felt like oil on her skin – unwanted, invasive. She shifted subtly away from him on the couch.

"Hey, brought my camera along," Brian cut in, reading the room. He lifted his well-worn DSLR. "Thought we could get some group shots in the snow."

Alice beamed at him, squeezing his hand. "You're so talented with that thing." The genuine affection in her voice was a stark contrast to the earlier tension.

"That'd be perfect, Brian." Scott sat up straighter, eager for the subject change. "Been too long since we've had decent pictures of everyone together."

They arrived at the base of the mountain which looked busier than anything else in the area. Skiers and snowboarders of all ages and skill levels milled about, their faces flushed with excitement. The group grabbed their equipment and headed for the lifts. David had already prepaid for the rentals. It took a minute for Emily to get used to the feeling of the skis under her feet, but it soon became almost natural.

The ski lift swayed gently as Scott bounced his leg, practically vibrating with excitement. Emily bit back a smile, charmed by his barely contained enthusiasm. The morning sun caught his dark hair as it whipped across those striking blue eyes, and her stomach did a little flip that had nothing to do with the height.

"I haven't been skiing in years," he confessed, his grin infectious. "This is going to be awesome."

Emily laughed, the crisp mountain air slowly replacing her jitters with anticipation. "Me neither. God, I hope muscle memory is real."

"Ah, you'll do great," he said, bumping her shoulder with his. "Just don't fall."

"Easy for you to say, Simmons." She raised an eyebrow at him.

"What, would you rather be snowboarding?"

"Absolutely not!" The giggle burst out of her. "At least skiing gives me a fighting chance. Put me on a snowboard and I'd face-plant before we even reached the top."

Scott's laugh echoed across the mountainside. "We'll stick together. That way when—not if—you fall, I can be there...to make fun of you."

"Oh, feeling pretty confident there, are we?" Emily narrowed her eyes playfully. "Care to race me?"

"I would," he drawled, eyes twinkling, "but I'd get so lonely..." He smirked. "You know, waiting at the bottom for half an hour until you finally appeared."

Emily rolled her eyes, but when Scott casually draped his arm across her shoulders, she found herself leaning into his warmth, the butterflies in her stomach doing their own kind of ski jumps.

The lift swayed gently as it carried them up the mountain. Emily noticed David sitting next to Alice in the front of the lift. They were engaged in an animated conversation, their laughter echoing despite the wind. Emily found this peculiar; she was unsure about the dynamic of their relationship. She didn't think they were friends, but she also didn't know much about David or what Alice had been up to the last few years. Emily decided to let it go and enjoy the day.

When they all got off, Alice appeared angry. She had just been laughing a moment before. Emily wondered if David said something, and she scooted on her skis over to Alice, hoping to salvage her joviality.

Before Emily could say anything, Alice put a hand up. "I just need a minute." Alice shook her head and wandered over to a small shop at the top of the mountain. Meanwhile, the rest of the crew prepared to venture on down, seemingly unaware one of them had wandered off.

Emily peeked through the window of the shop Alice had entered to see her wiping her face and heading to the restroom. For a moment she wondered if she should follow Alice, but didn't want to cross any boundaries, especially since they hadn't seen each other in so long. Emily decided to ignore it and continue with the ski day. She would catch up with Alice later.

David was right about the view from the top of the mountain. The slopes of Mount Riviera seemed like they belonged in another world, with powdery snow and stunning views stretching as far as the eye could see. Emily and Scott took their time taking in the views. Neither of them had ever seen anything like it, and it was a beautiful shared spectacle. The pair was more cautious on the first few runs while they got used to the feel of the skis beneath them. The group stuck together, laughing and shouting encouragement to one another as they sped down the mountain.

Claire and David were both naturals on skis, gracefully weaving between the trees. Claire shouted back at the group, "Come on, guys! Keep up!"

Brian, on the other hand, was more cautious. "I don't want to break anything," he called out, struggling to keep his balance. It was Brian's first time on skis, and he was certainly trying his best.

Mark, trying to show off, attempted a few tricks, much to Emily and Scott's amusement. Mark was pretty good at skiing even though he probably hadn't done it for as long as Emily had.

Smiling, Emily remembered long ago when her father took the family to a small resort and taught her how to ski. He was so patient with her.

"Show-off," Scott teased. Mark looked back at Scott and Emily and then nearly hit a tree.

Alice joined the group at some point without explaining why she had been gone. Alice glued her idiosyncratic face of joy. If Emily hadn't seen her crying just a short time before, she wouldn't have suspected anything was wrong.

Emily watched Alice carefully as they continued down the slope. Her friend's practiced smile was flawless—too flawless. Years of knowing Alice had taught Emily to recognize when that bright exterior was masking deeper turmoil. The way Alice's fingers fidgeted with her ski poles, how her laugh came just a beat too late at jokes, the slight tension in her shoulders—all tiny tells that something was very wrong.

She caught Alice stealing glances at Claire when she wasn't looking, but each time someone turned toward her, that megawatt smile would snap back into place, so convincing that Emily almost doubted what she'd seen.

Brian suddenly called out to the group, "Hey everyone, wait up!" He was fumbling with his camera, his photographer's eye clearly caught by something. "The light right now - it's perfect. The way the sun's hitting the snow..." He gestured enthusiastically. "We need a group shot."

"Really? Now?" Scott asked, but there was amusement in his voice rather than irritation.

"Trust me," Brian said, already positioning people with gentle guidance. "Alice, could you move just a bit to your left? The sun will catch your hair beautifully there." His face lit up as Alice complied with a laugh. "Perfect!"

Emily watched as Brian transformed, his usual reserved demeanor replaced by confident enthusiasm as he directed them. She had never seen him so animated, so in his element. Even Mark's typically surly expression softened as Brian's excitement proved infectious.

"Scott, relax your shoulders a bit," Brian called out. "This isn't a police lineup!"

Claire giggled while David wrapped an arm around her waist. The tension from the previous night's dinner seemed to melt away under the bright mountain sun.

"Okay, everyone ready?" Brian set up his tripod quickly, with practiced ease. He jogged over to join them, settling in beside Alice. "Three, two, one..."

The shutter clicked several times in rapid succession. Brian hurried back to check the results, and his face broke into a genuine smile. "These are perfect. I'll make copies for everyone."

Emily couldn't help but notice how natural Brian seemed in that moment - not an outsider at all, but a part of their group. His passion for photography had briefly brought them all together, creating a moment of pure joy in the trip. She made a mental note to ask Brian for a copy later - it would look perfect next to the photo of her and Scott on her desk at the library.

After a few hours of skiing and falling, the group decided to take a break near a bank of snow. The girls started building a snowman, and their laughter echoed through the trees. Out of the corner of her eye, Emily saw Mark making a snowball with a smug look.

"Hey, David, look out," Mark said through a mischievous grin as he threw the snowball. David ducked at the last second, and it just barely missed him. Instead, it hit the shop window, leaving a small crack in the glass.

"What the hell, Mark?" Claire shouted, her face flushing with anger.

"I—I'm sorry. It was just a snowball," Mark insisted, trying to look remorseful despite his barely hidden smirk. Laughter overcame him.

"There was a rock in that snowball, you ass. What were you trying to do?" David marched closer to Mark.

Scott stepped between them. "Hey, come on guys, relax. I'm sure it was an accident."

Claire rushed forward. "Honey, are you all right?" she ran to David's arms.

He calmly responded, "I'm fine. Just caught me off guard." He shook his head. "There's something wrong with that guy."

While everyone else returned to the cars, Emily lingered, watching as David entered the little shop. He paid the owner handsomely for the window before apologizing and shaking the man's hand.

Emily couldn't help but notice the way David's eyes remained on Alice as she walked away, a look of longing in his eyes. The interaction, coupled with the earlier tension between Alice and David on the ski lift, left Emily with a growing sense of unease. There was something not quite right about the situation, and she couldn't shake the feeling that there was more going on.

Back at the lodge, the group decided to explore the expansive property. The lodge was filled with concealed rooms that told stories of the past. One of the most fascinating they found was a game room of sorts. Poker chips scattered across green felt in the corner of the room, and in the center of the room a crimson billiards table. The walls were adorned with old, unsettling paintings. There were images of families from decades ago, their faces stern and unsmiling. Goosebumps formed on Scott's arm as he examined the artwork more closely.

Emily tapped Scott's shoulder and pointed to a portrait, her hands moving in fluid signs. "This place has so much history."

Scott signed back, "Yeah, and it's kind of creepy, don't you think?"

"Just because it's unfamiliar doesn't mean it has to be scary,"

"The family legacy was built on slave ownership, I don't know, just something about being surrounded by their faces-"

"Well, Scotty, if it makes you feel better, they are all buried six-feet underground."

He rolled his eyes with a smile, "You know I don't believe in ghosts or anything, I was just saying it's a little unsettling."

"I think you're more unsettled because you know I can kick your ass."

"Oh, we are definitely coming back here later and putting that to the test. Big talk," he signed with exaggerated movements.

"You can't play me right now? Don't tell me you're nervous, Simmons," she taunted.

"Oh I absolutely could, I just figured I'd give you some time to mentally prepare before losing so terribly to me. Come on, let's keep checking out these freaky rooms."

Emily's silent laugh lit up her face as she followed him into the hallway, enjoying their banter.

After wandering around for a bit, they found the rest of the group lounging around in the expansive library. Emily found a book coated in a thin layer of dust. It had nearly been hidden behind a pile of boxes and looked like it hadn't been touched in years. The cover was adorned with a small, hand-drawn purple heart. She picked up the book and carefully opened it, revealing yellowed pages filled with handwritten notes. The spine was stiff from years of abandonment. She couldn't help but wonder how old it was. The handwriting was elegant but difficult to read. Emily looked at it for some time, enraptured by the stories.

The words spoke to Emily as she flipped to a random page and read them to herself, "*I can't breathe. I can't speak. We can't let our hearts beat loud enough for them to hear.*" She continued flipping through the pages.

March 15, 1893

The voices grow louder with each passing day. Last night, I heard weeping from the servants' quarters, but when I went to investigate, the room was empty. Mary's old bed remained untouched, gathering dust. The other maids refuse to sleep there now.

William tells me the lodge has a way of knowing people's hearts. He says his grandfather built it with dark intentions, using wealth gained through unspeakable means. The stones themselves seem to hold memories. Sometimes, when I clean the library, books fall from shelves without being touched. The pages always open to accounts of tragedy—murders, disappearances, unexplained deaths.

I've started noticing changes in the family. Charles grows more volatile each day. His eyes follow me through rooms, and his smile reminds me of a predator sizing up prey. Even William seems different. Yesterday, I caught him staring at his reflection in the grand hallway mirror, but it wasn't his face I saw looking back. There was something else there, something hungry.

The other servants whisper that the lodge feeds on fear, growing stronger with each terror it witnesses. I used to dismiss such talk as superstition, but now I'm not so sure. The walls feel closer than before, and the shadows stretch longer, reaching for us with greedy fingers.

I should leave, but something holds me here. Perhaps the lodge has already claimed part of my soul, just as it claimed Mary's. I pray these words survive as a warning to others: this place changes people. It takes what's darkest in our hearts and brings it to the surface, drop by poisoned drop, until we drown in our own darkness.

Alice tapped on Emily's shoulder. "What does it say?" Her small frame was still enough to startle Emily from her concentration.

Emily squinted at the pages. "It's someone's diary. From the looks of it, it's really old. There's a lot about the weather and daily life ... but also mentions of strange occurrences. Listen to this: '*The howling at night continues. It keeps us all awake. The children are scared.*'"

"Spooky," Brian said jokingly.

Emily put the diary into her jacket pocket and joined the rest of the group. They continued exploring, discovering hidden nooks and crannies. Clothing from another era filled old trunks. They found antique furniture that seemed to belong to a different world. The more they explored, the more they realized how much history the lodge held and how much of it had been abandoned.

Scott wandered into a dimly lit hallway and found a door slightly ajar. He pushed it open to reveal a small room filled with broken furniture, hunting trophies, and countless weapons mounted on the walls. He felt a sense of unease but couldn't look away.

"Guys, you have to see this," Scott announced.

The group joined him, their faces changing as they walked into the room.

"Who needs this many weapons?" Scott muttered as he wandered around the space.

Mark examined a rifle mounted on the wall. "These guns look like they haven't been touched in years. Kinda *awesome*."

"*Weapons*," Scott corrected, sounding more like a teacher than a peer. "Guns are *toys*, weapons are *tools*." His law enforcement experience was painfully obvious.

The air was starting to feel a bit stale. The taxidermied animals seemed to stare back at Emily with accusing eyes, their lifeless forms a haunting symbol of the lodge's hunting legacy.

"Trust me, I know David's family has a very long history of weird rich people." Claire's voice was a bit strained as she tried to maintain her cheerful facade. "Let's head back to the living room. I think we all could use a little break."

Emily couldn't shake the feeling in the pit of her stomach. She had started to feel a heaviness in every room, even in the ones that seemed harmless. Emily hoped the others weren't having the same feelings.

Back in the living room, they gathered around the fireplace, the warmth of the fire a welcome contrast to the chilly atmosphere of the lodge. They settled into the comfortable couches, the tension from the morning's ski outing thankfully giving way to a much more relaxed mood.

"All right, who's up for a game?" Claire asked, shuffling through a deck of cards. David gathered a bottle of wine from a nearby cabinet.

The group agreed with nods of approval and an "I could use a drink," from Mark. Emily stuck to a glass of water as they settled around the coffee table.

"Have you guys played spoons?" Claire asked, making sure to face Emily as she spoke.

Brian asked, "Is that the one with the cards and you grab the-"

Alice and Mark looked entirely confused.

"Here, I'll explain," Claire said, dealing four cards to each player as David returned with wine and placed six spoons in the center of the table - one fewer than the number of players. "Everyone gets four cards. The goal is to get four of a kind, like four sevens or four kings."

Mark studied his cards. "What about four cards that are all the clovers?"

"The clovers are clubs, Mark, and no, the suit doesn't matter." Claire said with sisterly exasperation. "I'll pass cards to my left. When you get a card, you can keep it by trading it with one in your hand, or pass it along. Whoever gets four matching numbers first grabs a spoon. If you see someone grab one, you better be quick - there's one less spoon than players."

"Like musical chairs," Scott signed and spoke simultaneously.

"Exactly. Everyone ready?"

The game began, cards flowing rapidly around the circle. Mark's brow furrowed as he struggled to keep pace. Emily, however, had a strategy. Three fives already sat in her hand - hearts, clubs, and diamonds. She discarded everything else, waiting for the specific card she needed.

When Alice passed the five of spades, Emily's hand flashed out, smoothly snatching a spoon without drawing attention. Scott, ever observant, noticed the subtle movement and grabbed one next. A chain reaction followed: Brian, then Alice, then David lunged for the remaining spoons, leaving Mark empty-handed.

Mark threw his hands up in defeat and gathered the cards to shuffle for another round, while good-natured laughter rippled through the group.

As the games and banter continued, David excused himself and headed towards the hallway they had explored earlier. Curiosity piqued, Emily decided to follow him discreetly. She found him in the small room with the hunting trophies, staring at the large painting above the fireplace. The oil painting depicted three Victorian-era hunters standing over their quarry—a magnificent stag whose throat had been torn open, its dark blood staining the winter snow beneath. The men's faces were twisted in expressions of almost obscene pleasure, their clean white shirts spattered crimson. Emily cringed and turned her attention to David. His family had owned the lodge for generations, so Emily couldn't imagine the stories he grew up hearing. In fact, he probably knew stories of the men in the painting.

"Hey, David. You okay?" Emily asked softly, hoping she wasn't startling him. She had to remember David wasn't as adept at sign language as most of the group, so she tried to keep it simple.

David turned, a troubled look in his eyes. "I guess I just needed a short moment alone. I was just... thinking." His face was clouded with thoughts he couldn't shake.

Emily reached out and placed a comforting hand on his arm. She didn't know what was going on, but she wanted to help. "If you ever want to talk, I'm here. Deaf people can be terrific listeners," she chuckled. "Or if you want me to go away, I can do that, too."

"This place used to be my escape, you know?" His eyes drifted to the ornate portraits lining the walls, each face a reminder of his burden. "I've spent years trying to build something different, something better. But being here..." He swallowed hard. "Every painting, every fixture in this lodge was bought with money they took from honest people. Three generations of Belmonts who thought they could own everything and everyone."

Emily had never heard the stories of the Belmont family. Only that David had single-handedly rebuilt their fortune. She nodded sympathetically, waiting for him to continue.

"I just wish Claire had told me everyone was coming. It's not that I don't want you all here, but..." He gestured at the portraits surrounding them. "Sometimes I need time to prepare. To face all of this. The lodge is beautiful, preserved perfectly, but that's almost worse. It's like a museum dedicated to everything I'm trying to move past."

"No one is going to blame you for taking some time to yourself," Emily assured him. "I tend to step away and get lost in a book for a few hours—helps when I'm overwhelmed."

David gave her a small, genuine smile, though the weariness never left his eyes. "Thanks, Emily. That means a lot." He nodded, and they left the room together.

They returned to the living room where the rest of the group was still engrossed in their game. The bottle of wine was nearly empty, and Scott's heavily mumbled words showcased his drunkenness. Emily didn't often see him drink; it was humorous and refreshing to see him loosen up.

As the evening wore on, the group decided to call it a night. They said their goodbyes and headed to their respective rooms. Emily decided to hang back on the couch to look at the fire for a bit. She liked the idea of sitting alone for a bit.

A glass or two—Emily couldn't remember—of wine later, she saw a slight shuffling of feet to her right.

"Mark!" Emily smacked the couch a bit too excitedly. She realized she may have had too much to drink. "Come sit with me."

Emily knew they hadn't had a chance to even say hi to Mark, and she thought if she waited until she was sober, she might not get her chance to clear the air with him.

"Hey, Ems," Mark stepped into the firelight. "I was just getting some water."

Emily laughed more than the comment warranted, and she covered her mouth, ashamed, knowing the wine was affecting her.

"I'm gonna get you some water, too," Mark signed.

Emily stared at the fire trying to center herself. Before this trip she hadn't had alcohol in a very long time, and she didn't want to embarrass herself. Especially not in front of Mark.

Mark returned quickly with the water. Two ice cubes clinked against the walls of the glass. Emily laughed to herself thinking about how water is just melted ice. Mark didn't find her realization as funny as she did.

"Thank you," Emily signed. "Do you want to sit down?"

Mark sat on the couch a few feet away from Emily and leaned forward to put his glass on the table before getting comfortable.

Mark stared straight ahead at the fire. "Are you enjoying the trip?" He was gentle with his words as if he were afraid to say anything.

Maybe he should be afraid to say anything, Emily thought. *I kind of still hate him.*

Emily had loved Mark with the intensity of any first love, her heart aching for his touch, her soul yearning for his affection. She remembered the stolen glances, the bashful smiles, the secret kisses in the trees of the schoolyard. But the wounds of the past had never fully healed.

Looking at Mark's shadow in the fire, Emily couldn't bring herself to be angry. Maybe it was the wine, but all she could see was the gentle boy she loved in high school.

"It's been good," Emily replied honestly. "It's been nice seeing everyone."

Mark's face turned puzzled.

Emily chuckled, "Yes, even you." She hesitated before continuing, "You know, I really should be mad at you."

"Emily ..."

"I've had a lot of time to think these past ten years since you *cheated on me.*"

"Emily, we were practically children—"

Before Emily could even process what Mark had said, his head jerked toward the doorway to the foyer. Scott had appeared with a bag of chips and a charming grin. "Scott," Emily began. *Join us,* she wanted to say, but she realized it may not be the best idea. Instead, she signed, "What are you doing awake?"

Scott replied, "I noticed you weren't in your room. I wanted to see—" he stammered, "—if you wanted to chat? I'm sorry. I don't mean to interrupt anything." Scott's mannerisms remained innocent, but to Emily's confusion, his eyes showed a glimmer of hurt.

Emily stood and tried not to make her glaring at Mark obvious. "I'm sorry, Scott," Emily said as she walked past him. "I'm a little drunk, and I think I just need to take a walk."

Emily, feeling a mix of exhaustion, curiosity, and a significant buzz from the wine, decided to take one last look around the lodge before turning in. She could have used some sleep, but she couldn't stop thinking about the figure standing in her doorway last night.

Emily was drawn to the lodge's extensive library. How could she not be? The more she explored the room, the more she learned it was a treasure trove of knowledge, with floor-to-ceiling bookshelves overflowing with volumes that spanned centuries. Emily ran her fingers along the spines of the books, feeling the smooth leather and imagining the stories within.

As she explored, she discovered a hidden alcove behind a sliding bookshelf. Pushing the doors open, a vibration went up Emily's arm and through her veins. Emily jerked her hand back and peered inside. Inside were old letters and photographs yellowed with age and strewn about like a twister had arrived just before she had.

Emily remembered the diary she had found previously which she had been carrying around with her. She hadn't looked at it much because it gave her chills to even think about it. Emily dug the book out of her pocket and started reading from the beginning this time, hoping to uncover more clues about the lodge's past.

The inside cover was detailed with curly letters spelling the name "Lily." Emily soon learned that Lily was a maid for the Belmont family in the early 1890s. The first few pages mentioned starting work at the lodge and meeting the Belmont family. Eventually, it detailed strange noises at night, the feeling of being watched, and entries about being told to ignore it. Emily's heart raced as she read on, the sense of foreboding growing with each entry.

Aspen, Colorado – Winter, 1892

The people stare and chatter. Not at me—at the walls. The place is quiet until night. I asked Mr. Belmont about the noises, and he struck me in the face. "Asking questions like that will do you more harm than good," or "Maids don't speak unless spoken to," he would say. So I sweep the floors and mop the kitchen and don't speak unless I'm spoken to.

William is nice to me. He is the only one who lets me call him anything besides Mr. or Mrs. Belmont. I still look down when he speaks to me, but he at least lets me smile. I like to clean now because William tells me when I do a good job.

William tells me the noises are real. This lodge has a way of making good people great, and evil people worse.

Suddenly, a light flickered on in Emily's periphery, and she turned to see Scott standing in the doorway, his expression serious.

"Emily, are you okay? You've been in here for a while," he said, his eyes filled with concern.

Emily took a deep breath, closed the diary, and returned it to her jacket pocket. "Yeah, I'm fine. Just got caught up in this diary. It's ... unsettling, to say the least." Emily was hesitant to address the diary entries. She didn't want to startle anyone before she knew more.

Scott stepped closer, his eyes scanning the room. "This whole place is a little unsettling, to be honest. There's something not right here, and I think we need to be careful."

Emily appreciated Scott's concern and nodded in agreement. "You're right. We need to stick together and keep an eye out for anything unusual." Emily had hoped the feelings she was getting were unique to her, as she wanted everyone else to enjoy their time together. Though, it was surprisingly comforting to know she wasn't the only one getting a weird feeling.

Scott placed a reassuring hand on her lower back. "You'll tell me if you want to go home, okay?"

Feeling the warmth in Scott's presence, Emily smiled. "Thanks, Scott. I'm glad you're here."

They left the library together, the diary's secrets lingering in Emily's mind. As they made their way to their rooms, Emily couldn't shake the feeling that the lodge held more mysteries than they had anticipated. The events of the day had only deepened her sense of unease, and she knew that the coming days would reveal even more about the lodge. She knew that they had to be careful and that the answers they sought might not come easily.

Emily felt a knock on her door after she had already gotten into her night clothes which were honestly more skin than fabric. Wrapping a blanket around her half-exposed frame, she opened her bedroom door to see Scott with a couple of glass mugs.

Emily smiled and waved Scott in. "What's up?" Emily asked cheerfully, grabbing one of the mugs from Scott's hands.

"I thought we could use a break after such a dramatic day." His hands were slightly shaking, but he was smiling. Emily figured he might be nervous about something.

Scott seemed like he was trying not to look right at her.

"Oh." She looked down at her exposed stomach. "Let me put on a shirt." Emily threw a baggy shirt over her pajamas.

Sitting on her bed, she took a sip from the mug. "Oh! Not tea," she said as Scott laughed. She had never drunk this much in her life. Playfully, he gestured to clink their mugs together.

"To us," Emily smiled, leaning her head on Scott's shoulder.

Scott and Emily giggled in her room for close to an hour before he suggested they play truth or dare. Emily shook her head at the smirk spreading across his face. He looked so happy, and it made Emily feel the same way. They sat across from each other, cross-legged with their knees almost touching.

After a few playful rounds and shared drinks, Emily chose *truth*. The drinks swirled in her head. She had a nice buzz going and wondered if Scott was tipsy, too.

"What do you think about me?" she asked softly.

Scott took a deep breath and smiled, pushing a strand of hair behind Emily's ear. "I think I'm in love with you."

Emily knew he loved her as a friend, but the way he said it then had an edge of urgency. Emily paused and focused on what he was saying.

"Are you saying this because you're drunk?" Emily asked. Really she knew he was being honest. She could always tell in his eyes.

Scott grabbed Emily by the shoulders and looked her in the eyes. "I'm in love with you."

Emily knew, without a shadow of a doubt, that he meant it. She pulled him into a hug and felt better than she had this entire trip.

Emily knew she loved Scott too; she was just scared of losing the first friend she ever had and scared of letting herself be vulnerable. At that moment, though, she wanted to be vulnerable. She had longed to be loved this way her entire life.

CHAPTER THREE—Jealousy

Saturday

Emily awoke still wrapped up in the gentleness of her dreams, the weight of the night still hanging thick in the air. In a good way, this time. Emily smiled and walked across the hall to Scott's bedroom. When she entered, he was already awake and fully dressed. She ran to give him a hug. He tightened his grip around her frame and kissed the back of her head, sending chills down Emily's spine. It was clear that, sober, he felt the same as he had last night.

Downstairs, the aroma of coffee and breakfast hit her before she even reached the kitchen. David, Alice, and Brian sat clustered around the kitchen island, their plates half-empty. She pulled out a stool and slid onto it.

Meredith lifted the coffee pot. "Need a cup?"

Emily blinked, Scott's words from last night still echoing in her mind. "God, yes."

"Last night was awesome," David said between bites. "We should make game night a regular thing."

"Count me in," Scott chimed in.

Emily kept her eyes fixed on her coffee. Their usual playful banter suddenly felt loaded after last night's conversation – one she definitely hadn't been ready for.

Trying to break the tension, she glanced around. "Claire not up yet?"

"Still sleeping," David said with a shrug, taking another sip.

Emily's eyebrows shot up. "Claire? I didn't think *Mrs. 5AM* was capable of that," Laughing softly, she took her coffee and headed upstairs.

At the master bedroom door, she knocked gently. "Hey Claire?" Silence answered.

Inside, she found Claire sprawled in bed, headphones firmly in place. The sight startled Emily—this disheveled version of her friend was a far cry from the Claire she knew, who wouldn't dream of facing the day without perfect makeup and a coordinated outfit. Emily approached the bed carefully.

Claire yanked off her headphones at Emily's knock, fingers running through her tangled hair. "Oh... Emily."

"Rough night?" She signed, still hovering in the doorway.

"Just needed some beauty sleep, I guess." Claire's attempt at a laugh came out hollow.

"Had to make sure you weren't dead down here." Emily smiled, trying to lighten the mood.

"Alive, barely." Claire winced. "Don't drink more than three glasses of pinot."

"Noted." Emily studied her friend's face. "You sure you're okay? Everyone's downstairs. Last day and all."

"Yeah, I figured." Claire shrugged, not quite meeting her eyes. "Didn't really have plans anyway. Thought we'd just wing it."

"Want to join us downstairs?"

"Let me take a quick shower." Claire swung her legs over the bed, movements sluggish. "I'll be down."

Emily lingered in the doorway for a moment before heading out. Something was definitely off – Claire seemed more bothered than hungover. But if she wasn't ready to talk, Emily wouldn't push. Some things needed time.

The rest of the day seemed to fly by. Emily and Scott spent hours outside trying to build an igloo, but it was becoming nearly impossible with the snow rising as quick as it was. The storm was brewing over them, just a day before their drive home.

Inside, Claire and Mark were on the phone with their parents—a video call that Mark seemed very uninterested in. Emily ran upstairs to dry off and get changed into warmer clothes when she heard David and Alice talking in the hallway. Just as she felt like an interruption to even walk between them, Alice left David's company to join Emily.

"Hey girly," Alice said, cheerfully.

"Hey! I feel like I haven't gotten to spend that much time with you!" Emily replied with a friendly smile.

"Uh-yeah, probably because you've only been talking to *Mr. Police Man*." Alice cracked up laughing.

"Hey!" Emily smacked Alice's arm. "At least I'm not running around with a married man!"

Alice's face shifted. "What are you talking about?"

"Ah, I'm just kidding," Emily responded, but something in the air had changed.

Alice sat on Emily's bed while she changed out of her snow clothes. The silence between them felt heavier than usual.

"Ugh, the reception is so spotty up here." Alice rolled her eyes, staring at her phone.

Emily tried to keep the conversation light. "How's Brian enjoying the trip so far? I know Mark can be a jerk."

Alice shrugged, her attention elsewhere. "I think he's doing alright. He's been off taking pictures everywhere."

"Oh yeah? I've seen some of his stuff online, he's really talented."

Alice smiled, but it didn't quite reach her eyes. "I think Meredith is making something good downstairs. I can smell it." She was already shifting away from the topic.

Emily watched her friend carefully. This wasn't the Alice she knew—the one who could talk for hours about nothing and everything. Instead, she seemed distant, lost in thoughts she wasn't ready to share.

Half-starved from their day, the group piled into the dining hall of the Belmont Lodge. The room took their breath away. A massive wooden table stretched through the center, its surface polished smooth and glowing in the light. Old hunting trophies and paintings hung on the walls, telling stories of the lodge's past.

The table looked like something out of a magazine—fancy plates on crisp white tablecloths, shining silverware, and crystal glasses that caught the light from the chandelier above. Wonderful smells filled the air: roasted chicken fresh from the oven, creamy garlic mashed potatoes, asparagus, and warm bread that made their mouths water. It all mixed perfectly with the rich scent of the red wine Claire had picked out for their dinner.

As the group gathered around the table, Emily took her seat next to Scott, happy to rejoin him even after just twenty minutes. Across the table, Mark sat with his head down, his eyes occasionally meeting hers before quickly darting away. He was like a pathetic dog. The tension between them was strong, a silent reminder of their questionable relationship and their short but lingering conversation in front of the fire the night before. Emily wondered if she was the only one still thinking about it. Based on Mark's demeanor, she figured not.

Alice and Brian sat next to each other, their hands intertwined. They seemed oblivious to the tension in the room, their conversation filled with laughter and whispered secrets. Meredith moved around the table, serving the food and topping off glasses. Claire and David seemed to be playing roles—the perfect hosts. Their smiles were warm and welcoming, but Emily noticed something strained beneath the surface. Like actors who had rehearsed their lines too many times.

"To old friends and new memories," Claire said, raising her glass. "It's been so wonderful to have us all together again."

"To old friends," the group echoed, clinking their glasses. The initial clink was followed by the soft murmur of conversation. Emily filled her mouth with the soft song of red wine.

"So, Emily," Brian began, "how's the library these days? I heard you've been doing some amazing work with the community." He hadn't spoken much since they all arrived, so it was nice of him to ask.

Emily smiled, grateful for the light topic. "It's been great. We've started a new program for children, and the turnout has been wonderful. We've seen so many kids improve their reading scores with our program."

"That's fantastic," Alice said, her eyes sparkling. "You really are making a difference."

Scott, always eager to support Emily, added, "She's crushing it. The whole town loves her."

Emily felt a sweet thump in her chest at Scott's words. She elbowed him gently while she blushed, and they continued their meal.

Mark swirled his wine glass. "Meanwhile, you two are living the Manhattan dream. Your rent probably costs more than my house."

"We manage," Brian said vaguely.

Alice speared an asparagus stalk. "Our closet-sized palace is quite cozy, thank you very much."

"Are you planning to stay in the city?" Scott asked between bites.

Brian and Alice exchanged a look. "Actually," Brian started, "I've been thinking California might be nice. Better for my photography, you know?"

Alice's fork stopped halfway to her mouth. "California?" Her tone was light, but her eyes narrowed. "First I'm hearing of this."

"Just thinking out loud." Brian backpedaled.

"No, no, California's great." Alice's smile was tight. "We've just never talked about it, ever."

Scott cleared his throat. "Hey, Claire, this chicken is incredible."

"Oh, that was all Meredith." Claire waved off the compliment. "I just watched and handed her things."

As the meal progressed, the conversation continued, but beneath the surface, there were undercurrents of tension. Between bites of the lavish meal, Emily noticed Mark's jaw tighten whenever Scott spoke, and Claire seemed unusually quiet. Claire's eyes danced between David and Alice, her face narrowing with suspicion whenever they interacted. She wasn't even being subtle about it.

As if everyone could sense the growing tension and were trying to avoid it, they turned the conversation to their careers. Alice spoke passionately about her current work in marketing, her ambition evident in her every word. Brian, the enigmatic photographer, shared stories of his travels and the people he had met along the way. Claire and David talked about their real estate empire, their voices filled with pride and ambition. Scott, the humble policeman, spoke of the dangers and rewards of his job.

Emily followed along intently, fascinated by the different paths her friends had taken. It was amazing to discover who everyone had become after high school and know their dreams had come true.

Despite their best efforts, the tension in the room grew into a silent awkwardness beneath their polite conversation. A knot of anxiety tightened in Emily's chest. She had hoped this reunion would be a chance to reconnect with her old friends, to rekindle the bonds of their shared past. But it was becoming increasingly clear that the past was not as far behind them as they had hoped.

Scott leaned over to sign something secretly to Emily. "This wine is good, but I kind of want another *toddy* like we had last night."

Emily replied with a giggle and a nod of agreement.

Suddenly, Mark set his fork down and leaned back in his chair, fixing Scott with a challenging stare. "You know, Scott, I've been thinking about the *good old days*. Remember that championship basketball game? The one you *stole* from me?"

Scott looked up, surprised. "*Stole* from you? What are you talking about?"

"You know exactly what I'm talking about," Mark said, his voice rising slightly. "You hogged the ball and took all the glory for yourself. We could have won as a team, but of course, it had to be all about you."

Emily felt her stomach churn. She glanced around the table and saw the others shifting uncomfortably in their seats. The happy atmosphere had evaporated, replaced by a thick tension that hung heavy in the room. *This* Mark seemed more like the one Emily was used to.

"Mark, that was a long time ago," Emily said gently. "Let's move on."

"Doesn't change what happened," Mark retorted, his eyes never leaving Scott's.

Scott let out a deep breath, trying to keep his cool. "Mark, I'm sorry if you felt that way. It was high school basketball, I was always just doing my best for the sake of the team."

Mark scoffed, pouring himself another glass of wine. "You're the one who got all the praise. You got everything, asshole." Mark looked so quickly at Emily as he said the last few words that she was certain she imagined it.

The room fell into an uneasy silence, the only sound the crackling of the fire. Emily had a feeling Mark's sudden outburst was about something other than the ball game.

Claire stood up abruptly, breaking the spell. "How about some dessert? I made chocolate pie."

The group hesitantly resumed their conversation, steering clear of the earlier conflict, but the tightness remained. Claire's eyes continued darting between her husband and Alice.

"Is everything alright, Claire?" Alice asked, her voice laced with concern and a bit of annoyance from Claire staring at her.

Claire hesitated for a moment and then forced a smile. "Everything's fine, guys. Just a little tired, that's all."

But Emily wasn't convinced. She could see the turmoil in Claire's eyes. Unspoken words hung heavy.

As the evening wore on, Emily wanted nothing more than to dismiss everyone from the table. Claire's behavior became more erratic, her laughter forced and her smiles strained. She barely touched her dessert. About to explode, Claire slammed her hand on the table, the sound echoing through the room. "I've had enough of this!" she exclaimed, her voice shaking.

Everyone turned to look at her with shock and confusion. The group looked like they wanted to run.

"What's wrong, Claire?" David said gently. He rubbed his wife's arm.

Claire's eyes narrowed, her gaze fixed on Alice. "You know what's wrong, David. You and Alice. Don't think I haven't noticed the way you two have been acting."

Alice's face paled, and she looked at David who seemed equally surprised. "Claire, what in the hell are you talking about?"

"Don't you play dumb with me, Alice," Claire exclaimed. "I've seen the way you look at him. The way you follow him from room to room. You're trying to steal my husband from me!"

The room fell into a stunned silence. The incrimination hung in the air, heavy and suffocating. Alice's eyes filled with tears, and she shook her head vehemently. "No, Claire, that's not true. I have no interest in destroying a marriage, or cheating on Brian."

But Claire was beyond reason. "I'm not blind, Alice. I see the way you two are together. You're always whispering, always laughing. You think I don't notice?"

Brian, silent until now, reached out and took Alice's hand. "Claire, you shouldn't jump to conclusions. Alice and I are happy together. Nothing is going on between her and David."

Claire continued, "Oh, really? Then why were you two alone on the ski lift yesterday? Why were you whispering and giggling like a couple of teenagers? Why have I walked in on you two alone in different rooms of this damn lodge several times since we've been here?"

Alice's face flushed with anger. "We were just talking, Claire. We've been getting along. There's nothing else to it."

"I don't believe you," Claire said, her voice cold and accusing. "I've seen that look you keep giving him."

The argument escalated. Allegations flew back and forth like poisoned darts. Emily and Scott exchanged worried glances, unsure of how to intervene. Mark sat in stony silence as he watched the drama unfold. Emily remembered the previous morning on the mountain when she saw Alice leave to cry after talking to David. There was at least *something* going on, but Emily knew it wasn't her business.

David, who had been trying to remain calm, finally spoke up. "Ladies, please. Let's not let this ruin our evening. We're all friends here."

But his words did not matter. Claire and Alice were too consumed by their anger and hurt to listen to reason.

"You stay out of this, David!" Claire snapped. "This is between Alice and me."

Alice turned on Claire, her eyes blazing. "You're right, Claire. This is between us, yet you brought it up in front of everyone. Accusing me of something terrible. Where do you get off? We are supposed to be friends."

With that, Alice stormed out of the dining room, her heels clicking against the hardwood floor. Brian trailed behind her, shoulders hunched in humiliation., leaving the rest of the group stunned in silence.

Emily looked at Scott, shocked at the outbursts. "What was that all about?" she asked, hoping he knew more than she did.

Scott shook his head. "I don't know, but it doesn't look good."

David, face pale, stood and excused himself from the table. "Claire and I need to talk," he whispered. David nodded, signaling Claire to follow him.

Claire watched him go, her eyes filled with tears and embarrassment. She turned to Emily and Scott. "First thing tomorrow morning, I want that woman *out* of this house."

Emily reached out, took Claire's hand, and offered a comforting squeeze. "I know you're upset, but come on. You know Alice."

"I don't know, Emily. Sometimes you just have to trust your gut when something is off." She took a breath before turning to the rest of the table. "I'm sorry I ruined the reunion guys. I enjoyed having you all stay here."

Emily could see the pain in Claire's eyes, the fear that her friendship with Alice, and potentially her marriage to David, were both irreparably hurt. Emily wanted to offer some kind of comfort, but she felt that nothing she could say would ease Claire's paranoia.

The rest of the evening was strained and awkward. Mark remained silent, his eyes fixed on the fire. Scott tried to make small talk, but his efforts fell flat. Emily could feel the flinging insults whispering around like moths' wings.

As the night wore on, the group dispersed. Each person retreated to their rooms with their thoughts and worries. It seemed like everyone had a headache. Emily lay awake in bed. The events of the evening replayed in her mind—the tears, the hurt. A shadow was cast over their reunion.

The aftermath of the dinner party left a bitter taste in everyone's mouths.

Alice in particular was deeply affected by the events of the evening. The assumption of infidelity, even if unfounded, had struck a nerve, exposing deep-seated insecurities.

She had always been the queen bee, the center of attention, the one everyone admired and envied. But beneath the facade of confidence and success, Claire harbored a gnawing fear of inadequacy, a constant worry that she wasn't good enough, that she didn't deserve the life she had.

These insecurities had been amplified by her marriage to David, a man who seemed to have it all—wealth, charm, intelligence, and seemingly effortless charisma. Claire loved David deeply, but she couldn't shake the feeling that she was constantly competing with him, that she had to prove her worth to him every day.

Alice's presence at the lodge had only exacerbated these feelings. Alice's youthful beauty and carefree spirit represented everything Claire feared she was not. She was spontaneous, adventurous, and seemingly immune to the anxieties and doubts that plagued Claire.

Since Alice's arrival a few days before the rest of the group, Claire's suspicions had grown. She had watched David and Alice interact. Her eyes had searched for any sign of intimacy or connection that went beyond friendship. She had seen them laughing together, sharing inside jokes, and exchanging glances that excluded her.

Her mind conjured up scenarios of betrayal and heartbreak. She imagined David and Alice sneaking off together, their laughter echoing through the lodge's empty halls. She imagined them in each other's arms, in her bed, their passion compared to the lukewarm affection she felt from David.

The more she thought about it, the more convinced she became that her suspicions were justified. She began to withdraw from the group, spending more time with Mark or alone in her room, brooding over her perceived betrayal.

David, sensing her distance, tried to reach out to her, but she rebuffed his attempts at intimacy. She couldn't bear to look at him, to see the love in his eyes that she feared was no longer hers.

As the day turned into night, Claire's paranoia grew. She began to see threats and conspiracies everywhere. Her mind twisted every innocent interaction into a sign of betrayal. She became convinced that David and Alice were plotting against her, that they were waiting for the right moment to reveal their affair and destroy her life.

Since Emily hadn't gotten a chance to talk about the previous night, she knocked on Scott's door. Emily then opened the door a crack, and Scott looked up at her. He looked exhausted but perked up when Emily entered.

"Hey, you," he said, patting the space beside him on his bed.

Emily's cheeks blushed without meaning to, and she signed quickly, "So, tonight got weird."

Scott rolled his eyes, attempting to forget the many outbursts from dinner. "Hey, tomorrow's our last day here. How about we say goodbye in the morning and head out a little early?" he suggested.

"I was thinking the same thing" Emily scratched her head, "the reunion was pretty fun but I'm ready to go home."

Scott smiled, pulling Emily's head to his chest and into a firm hug.

"You know I have feelings for you, too, Scott. I'm sorry I didn't actually say it last night and that might have been weird, but even without the drinks, I still feel the same way."

Scott seemed relieved at her words. "I was thinking, maybe when we get back to Glenwood ..."

"Scott, I want to date you. I don't want to rush into anything, we're amazing friends, but I don't want to ruin our relationship for some stupid fling." Emily said, her mind made up.

Scott leaned in and kissed her passionately. It felt like relief—like finally letting out a breath she didn't know she'd been holding. With all the tension suffocating the lodge, this moment was an escape. Emily closed her eyes and thought about tomorrow's drive home with Scott, now her *boyfriend*.

Scott wrapped Emily into a hug and said, "As long as I get to be with you."

He turned off the lamp, and they drifted off to sleep in each other's arms. As the night deepened, the snowfall intensified. Ice crept across the windows, while a blanket of snow gradually enveloped the lodge. Oblivious to the storm outside, Emily and Scott slumbered peacefully, their shared warmth a refuge against the winter's chill.

CHAPTER FOUR—Alice

Sunday

Emily woke with a start, her heart pounding frantically in her chest like a caged bird desperate for escape. The remnants of another vivid nightmare clung to her consciousness with tenacious fingers—a chilling vision of a stranger lurking in her room, watching her with malevolent intent. This unsettling dream echoed the veiled tensions and cryptic conversations that had permeated the lodge's grand halls the previous evening.

Limbs trembling, she rose from the plush bed, her bare feet sinking into the thick, luxurious Persian rug. The exquisite softness beneath her toes provided a distinct change to the cold dread that gripped her heart.

Her eyes were drawn to the gilt-framed mirror on the wall. It reflected her pale, freckled face, her eyes wide with fear. The reflection seemed foreign to her as if the past day had already begun to transform her. Something about the morning didn't feel right; an inexplicable sense of foreboding felt like a heavy fog.

Emily made her way to the window. Her heart sank as she faced a solid wall of white—packed snow pressed against the glass like concrete. There was no view of the mountains anymore, no forest, not even the winding road they drove up. Just an impenetrable barrier of snow that had completely entombed their side of the lodge.

She glanced back at Scott, momentarily lost in thought. The rise and fall of his chest as he slept was a small comfort amid her growing unease. Without warning, Scott jolted awake, his body tensing as if electrified.

Emily's heart leaped into her throat, her pulse quickening at his sudden movement. Scott's eyes, usually warm and reassuring, were now wide with alarm. In one fluid motion, he ripped his robe off its hanger. The wooden rod clattered to the floor with a sound that seemed deafening in the tense silence.

"Someone's screaming," Scott told her, his voice tight with urgency. "We have to go."

The words hit Emily like a physical blow and sent a chill down her spine. Without hesitation, she followed Scott. Her bare feet hardly touched the cold wooden steps. Scott's demeanor had transformed instantly, his law enforcement instincts taking command. His posture was rigid, his movements precise and purposeful—harshly different than the relaxed man she had known just moments before.

The rush of panicked footsteps and frantic voices reverberated through the lodge, a chaotic symphony of fear and confusion that seemed to shake the very foundations of the building. Emily's heart was pounding, vibrating in her ears as her stomach dropped. Something had gone very wrong.

The unknown threat loomed large in her imagination, fueled by the fear that permeated the air. As she reached the bottom of the staircase, her eyes adjusting to the dim light of the early morning, she saw her group of friends huddled around the fireplace in the living room.

Their faces were etched with shock and horror, a tableau of fear that made Emily's blood run cold. The silence that had fallen over the group was broken by the soft crackling of the fire and the ragged, shallow breathing of the terrified guests. The portraits on the walls, their subjects dressed in the finery of a bygone era, seemed to judge the scene unfolding beneath them with cold, painted eyes.

With trembling legs threatening to give way beneath her, Emily pushed her way through the crowd. The warmth of bodies pressed close around her was suffocating, adding to the sense of claustrophobia that threatened to overwhelm her. Her heart was pounding so loudly she was sure everyone could hear it, the sound almost drowning out her huffing breath. As she reached the front of the group, the crowd parting before her like a dark sea, she saw a sight that made her veins turn to ice.

Alice, vibrant and glowing just hours before, lay motionless on the floor. Her eyes, once sparkling with mischief and joy, the vibrant blue that had always reminded Emily of clear summer skies was now dulled by the icy grip of death, lifeless and empty. Alice's face was frozen in a mask of terror, her lips parted in a silent scream that would never find a voice.

A deep, angry bruise formed a grotesque ring around Alice's delicate neck, a stark testament to the violent struggle that had ended her life. The purple and black discoloration stood out in harsh contrast against her pale skin, telling a story of desperation and fear in its final moments. A crimson trail that seemed almost black in the dim light seeped from her nostril. The sight was so terrifying, so utterly wrong, that Emily's mind rebelled against it, unable to fully process the horror before her.

Emily gasped, the cold breath painful in her throat. Her hand flew to her mouth, fingers pressing hard against her lips to stifle another scream that threatened to tear itself from her chest. The room seemed to tilt and sway around her, reality becoming fluid and untrustworthy.

Wave after wave of nausea washed over her, and she had to lock her knees to keep from collapsing. It was as if all the color had been drained from the world, leaving only this nightmarish scene in a clear focus.

The antique furniture, with its dark wood and ornate carvings, seemed to whisper secrets of its own. Emily was drawn inexorably to the fireplace, its flames dancing and twisting in a hypnotic ballet. The fire's destructive abilities made it that much more intriguing, and her mind uncomfortably wandered to darker thoughts.

Mark, face ashen and drawn, knelt beside Alice. His eyes, usually steady and calculating, were now filled with a grief and unbridled rage. His fingers, trembling slightly, searched for a pulse at Alice's neck, avoiding the brutal bruising. After a moment that seemed to stretch into eternity, he shook his head, his voice barely a whisper in the deathly quiet room. "She's gone. She's really gone." The words seemed completely unreal. As if a switch had been flipped, Mark's eyes turned to Scott, blazing with accusation. "I swear to God if you fucking did this—" The words were a growl, raw with emotion.

Scott raised his hand to Mark, his voice steady despite the tension that radiated from every line of his body. "Enough. We all love Alice. I am not going to stop until I get to the bottom of this. We need to search the lodge—every room, every corner. But no one goes alone." His words were meant to calm, but there was a feeling of suspicion beneath them—a warning as much as a plea for unity.

The coat rack nearby held the group's winter clothes. Emily's eyes fell on Alice's pink scarf, the one she had gotten from her grandmother when she was young. Alice would never wear it again. The sight of it made Emily's heart clench painfully in her chest. As she watched, Brian stepped forward and gently took the scarf from its hook. With trembling hands, he brought it to his face, inhaling deeply. The faint remnants of Alice's perfume clung to the soft fabric. The ghost of her presence brought tears to Brian's eyes.

Scott quickly organized them into pairs. "Claire, David, take the upper floors. Emily and I will check the game room and library. Mark, Brian, search this level—foyer, living room, kitchen. Document everything, Brian. Your camera might catch something we miss."

The pairs dispersed, each duo moving with shared purpose despite their private tensions. Upstairs, Claire's grasp on David's hand was white-knuckled as they moved from room to room. "I haven't forgiven you," she whispered, her voice catching. "What you did last night, in front of everyone..." She swallowed hard. "But right now, you're all I have. I need you to be here with me."

David squeezed her hand in response, his own voice thick with emotion. "I'm here. Whatever you need."

In the hallway, Emily and Scott moved methodically through the game room and library. Emily's eyes traced every detail—the way the pool cues hung perfectly aligned on the wall, leather-bound books arranged with pristine precision on their shelves. Nothing seemed disturbed, yet something felt wrong. Emily couldn't help but wonder about the mysterious entries in the diary she had glimpsed earlier. She made a mental note to find a moment alone to read more, convinced that its pages held crucial information.

The strange pictures on the walls seemed to hold ominous significance. It all pointed to an evil that extended far beyond a simple reunion of old friends. Emily felt as if she were standing on the edge of a vast conspiracy, one that had been years in the making. The lodge itself seemed complicit, its walls and floors creaking with the weight of ancient secrets.

Meanwhile, in the foyer and living room, Brian documented everything with his camera, the mechanical click of the shutter punctuating the heavy silence. Mark moved restlessly between the kitchen and living space, his movements growing increasingly agitated.

"I can't believe this is happening," Brian whispered, lowering his camera. "Last night, she was just..." His voice cracked.

Mark's response was cut short as he crouched near the sofa, his body tensing. "Hey!" he called out, voice edged with alarm. "Everyone needs to see this." The group gathered around as Mark carefully lifted a revolver from under the sofa. Scott's face was drained of color.

Emily recognized it immediately—it was Scott's revolver, the one he kept secured in his room upstairs. The implications hung heavy in the air: someone had been going through their belongings. Scott's eyes narrowed at Mark. "That was in my room." His voice was dangerously quiet. "How did you find this?"

The tension in the room ratcheted up several notches as Mark shifted uncomfortably under Scott's gaze. Scott carefully tucked the revolver into his waistband, his movements deliberate as his eyes swept the room, taking in every detail, every face.

Without another word, he gestured for Mark to follow him to the library. They needed to get to the bottom of this—starting with Mark.

Scott took charge of the room immediately, his presence filling the space. He gestured for Mark to sit while Emily positioned herself in a corner to take notes. "Walk us through your night," Scott said with a tone professional but not unkind. "We were in the dining room. Then at some point, you went to your room. Take it from there."

Mark's posture was tense, and his jaw was clenched. When he spoke, his voice was tight with barely suppressed annoyance. "I went upstairs, grabbed my clothes, and went down the hall to take a shower," he began, his words clipped and precise. He scoffed. "The water in my bathroom takes forever to warm up, so I like to use the one in Claire and David's room."

Emily sat in the corner of the room with her notepad. She focused not just on Mark's words but on his demeanor—the way his shoes tapped restlessly on the carpet, the tension in his shoulders. Any detail could be the key that unlocked this terrible mystery.

"I took a hot shower and then went to bed," Mark concluded, his tone suggesting the matter was closed.

Scott leaned forward slightly. His eyes never left Mark's face. "That's it?" he asked, his voice neutral.

"That's it," Mark replied. A note of defiance crept into his voice.

Scott, ever the professional, stood up and opened the door as if he were running a doctor's office rather than investigating a murder. "That's all we need from you then," he said and stepped out into the hall. He raised his voice slightly, calling out, "David, you're up next."

Mark left the room with his back bent as if under a great weight, and then David entered. Contrasting with Mark's barely contained aggression, David moved with a sense of obedience. The search upstairs with Claire seemed to have drained him, leaving him looking older and more worn than before.

"I—uh, you know, I had a bit of a tough night last night," David explained hesitantly. He ran a hand through his hair nervously. "Guess you could say I'm in the dog house."

Emily's lip dropped in confusion. "Dog house?" she asked, prompting him to elaborate.

"Yeah—uh, troubles with the wife," David said. His fingers nervously tapped in a row on the arm of his chair. "She seemed to think ... that I would ... that Alice and I—" He trailed off.

"It's all right, man. We heard about it at dinner," Scott assured him.

David tsked, relieved to be spared from further explanation. "Right, anyways, um ... she kicked me out of the room, so truth be told, I fell asleep, uh—about where you're sitting, Emily."

Emily's eyebrows shot up in surprise, and she couldn't help but scoot a bit in her chair. The thought sent a chill down her spine, of David spending the night in this very spot while just through the door Alice was meeting her tragic end.

"You slept downstairs last night?" Scott asked.

David nodded, visibly sweating now. Beads of perspiration dotted his forehead as he answered, "Yeah, I—uh, I did." He sniffled, a nervous tic that Emily noted. "Woke up here too, to my wife screaming, you know."

Emily continued taking notes privately, and her mind raced with the implications of David's story. If he had truly spent the night downstairs, he would have had easy access to where Alice was when she died. But it also meant he might be a useful witness.

Scott asked, "So did you see anything? Hear anything?"

"Absolutely not." David shook his head. "Can't hear a thing over my CPAP machine." He paused, a flush creeping up his neck. "Except Claire's screams, of course." The chuckle that followed was strained, hanging awkwardly in the air.

Scott got up to open the door again, ending David's interview. "Thanks, David," he said blankly.

As David left, his shoulders slumped with relief, Brian entered the room. His usual confident demeanor was nowhere to be seen, replaced by a nervous energy that set Emily on edge.

"You guys, I'm sorry. I wish I could be more help with this whole thing, but I don't know anything," Brian pleaded before Scott could even begin questioning him. His words tumbled out.

"It's all right, have a seat" Scott directed him. "Just tell us what you do know."

Brian nodded and took a deep breath to steady himself. "Well, last night was a bit of a fiasco, as you know. We went on a walk and had a bit of an argument."

"About?" Emily asked, her pen poised over her notes.

Brian wiped his eyes from tiredness. "Just that stupid shit that Claire was on last night. I've been cheated on before, and I—I just needed to know if it was true." He shakily reached for a tissue from the desk.

Scott leaned forward with an intense stare. "Well, was it true?" he pressed.

"She said no, but who knows?" Brian choked. "I just went to bed frustrated. Alice took off her makeup and got in the shower, I went to sleep and woke up to that screaming downstairs." He blew his nose into the tissue. It sounded like a trumpet in the quiet room. "That's it."

"Thank you, Brian," Scott said. Brian left the room, his movements jerky and uncertain.

The last person to come into the library for questioning was Claire. Her eyes were red-rimmed from crying, her usual poise shattered by the morning's events.

"You guys have to believe me. I had nothing to do with this," Claire cried as soon as she entered the room. Her desperate eyes locked onto Emily. "Emily—we've been friends for how long?"

Scott scooted his chair closer to Claire's, his manner softening slightly in the face of her distress. "Claire. We're not making any assumptions yet. Just tell us your side of the story."

Claire's eyes moved around the library carpet for a moment before she answered as if searching for the right words. When she spoke, her voice was barely above a whisper. "I know I made quite the scene last night. Afterward, I had a long talk with my husband. I'm not sure of anything right now, but I told him he would not sleep with me, not for a little while." She wiped the tears from her cheeks with trembling hands. "Mark came in to use the shower, nothing out of the ordinary. I slept fine, I guess. Woke up at my usual time, around 5 a.m., came downstairs for coffee, and that's when I found her."

A sob escaped her, muffled by her sleeve. "You gotta believe me, I thought she was hungover, maybe she fell asleep like that—" Another cry wracked her body and stole her breath. "I can't believe I'm saying this, but I think my husband—" Her words dissolved into unintelligible sobs, and her entire body shook with the force of her grief and fear.

Emily, moved by her friend's distress, reached out and grabbed Claire's hand. "Hey, take a deep breath, Claire," she said softly, her voice soothing. "It's all right, just breathe."

But Claire was beyond comfort. Her next words came out in a shout, raw and filled with anguish. "I think my husband killed Alice!"

Emily and Scott exchanged a shocked glance as the implications of Claire's words sank in. The investigation had taken a dark and unexpected turn, and Emily knew that things would never be the same again.

The lodge increasingly felt like a labyrinth of shadows and secrets, its walls whispering of danger and deceit at every turn.

When she looked at her friend, broken and sobbing before her, Emily felt the weight of responsibility settle on her shoulders. She realized that uncovering the truth would come at a great cost, but for everyone's sake, she had to see this through to the end.

CHAPTER FIVE—Blackmail

As the day wore on and Emily and Scott pressed on with their investigation, their resolve strengthened with a mounting sense of urgency. They were acutely aware of the ticking clock.

A killer posed a threat to everything they held dear.

"What's your take on this?" Scott asked concernedly.

"I don't think he did it," Emily replied with unexpected confidence. "Not David."

Perplexed by her certainty, Scott countered, "Claire was very vocal about her feelings. If David had something to hide that Alice knew about, it makes sense that he'd meet her in the middle of the night and *silence* her."

Emily shook her head. "Alice never slept with David. I really don't think she did. If there was no affair to begin with, why would he need to silence her?"

"I want to believe you, but this doesn't add up," Scott signed. "With him sleeping right down here, he had perfect access. How can you be so certain there was no affair?"

"I can't explain it. It's just a gut feeling," Emily signed, shrugging. "I need to talk to Claire and dig deeper."

"Want me to come with you?"

"No, I'll be fine,"

Without another word, Emily left the library and hurried up to the master bedroom. There, she found Claire on the bed, crying harder than Emily had ever seen anyone cry.

"Hey, hon," Emily stepped in gently. "I'm here."

Claire raised her head slightly, her voice thick with emotion. "I know you don't believe me. You probably think I killed her, right?"

Taken aback, Emily moved closer. "Claire, it's me. Talk to me. Please."

Claire wiped her eyes. "I've never seen him like this before—the way he acts around Alice. At home, I get stoic, sophisticated David who barely speaks, but around Alice?" She let out a bitter laugh. "He becomes this chatty social butterfly."

"Maybe it's just the alcohol," Emily signed. "It helps us all loosen up."

"Emily." Claire's voice cracked. "You've seen Alice. She is—" She paused, pain flickering across her face. "She *was* the most adorable little thing."

"Yes, and she was also a loyal friend who would never sleep with your husband."

Claire rose to shut the bedroom door, then retrieved a small white envelope from behind the bed frame. "Here," she said, her hand trembling as she held it out. "I found this in David's nightstand a few days ago."

"Claire—" Emily began, hesitating. "Going through your husband's things..."

"Just open it."

Inside, Emily found a note addressed to David. It was handwritten in all caps with dark red ink, a small lipstick print adorning the bottom.

DAVID, MEET IN THE BASEMENT AT MIDNIGHT TONIGHT. YOU KNOW YOU DESERVE IT.
XOXO, A

"Well?" Claire demanded, clearly expecting a stronger reaction from Emily.

After a moment of contemplation, Emily looked up. "I don't think this is a love letter," she said, rising from the bed. "I think it's blackmail."

"What are you talking about?"

"Just- we need to talk to him about this."

Downstairs, Emily showed the note to Scott. Then, they confronted David at the bar in the kitchen."David," Scott called, placing the note on the counter, "can you explain this?"

David buried his face in his hands. Claire, hands on hips, shouted, "What do you have to say for yourself, you bastard?"

To their surprise, David almost smiled. "Honey ..." he began, shaking his head, "is this why you thought I was sleeping with Alice?"

Claire stood dumbfounded, still convinced of his infidelity.

David turned on his stool to face the group. "I'm not having an affair," he confessed, his voice heavy. "I ... I'm a fraud."

The group stood in shocked silence until Claire demanded, "Go on, then."

David took a deep breath. "Yes, I'm a fraud. I got involved in some stupid dealings at work. I was going to stop, I swear, but someone found out. So I started paying for their silence."

"Who's been blackmailing you?" Scott asked, his police instincts kicking in.

"Meredith, our housekeeper," David revealed. "It was supposed to be a one-time thing, but I guess she got greedy. The first night everyone arrived here, she decided to demand more money."

"If it wasn't Alice, why did she sign the note with 'A'?" Claire snapped.

"'*A*' for Anonymous, dear," David explained wearily. "It doesn't matter now. If I thought a little insider trading would ruin my reputation, being mixed up in a cold-blooded murder is inevitably going to destroy me. My business is finished." With that, he rested his head on the countertop, the weight of his actions finally crashing down upon him.

Scott realized he had been completely ignoring someone who might have the missing pieces they needed. Meredith had been the perfect servant, slipping in and out of rooms unnoticed. *What was she really capable of?*

Emily and Scott entered the basement where Meredith was folding laundry to ask her some questions. "Hey, Meredith?" Scott said, trying not to sound too much like a police officer. "We need to talk with you. Can you come with us to the library?"

Meredith did not look intimidated in the least. She followed them up the stairs. Scott shut the library door.

"Can you explain this note?" Scott handed her the blackmail threat.

Meredith sighed. "Yeah, that was me." Emily was stunned by how readily she admitted to such a serious crime.

"Why did—" Scott started before Meredith cut him off.

"You know, I get paid *five dollars an hour?*" Meredith rolled her eyes. "Mr. Belmont is a very rich man. I find out something he doesn't want exposed, I make a little more money. That's all." She reached into her purse for a breath mint.

"Alright, well you know blackmail is illegal, right? You can't extort someone for money just because you need a raise."

"Fraud is also illegal, no?"

"The two don't cancel each other out. If you hit my car, I don't get to take your purse."

"Look," Meredith leaned forward in her seat, "I didn't kill her."

"You have to understand, with all of the sketchy behavior around you—you don't look so good right now."

"I don't give a shit how I look. I don't kill."

"Then tell us what you were up to last night."

She let out a disgusted sound. "I made dinner for you all, ate my food downstairs, and came back up at about nine to clean up. Usually I work with an entire crew, but this weekend I'm by myself. I go to sleep when Ms. Claire tells me she doesn't need anything else—last night that was around 11:30. My room is down in the basement. I was there all night."

"Did you get to interact with Alice at all this weekend?" Scott asked.

"Yeah, she was a lot more friendly than the rest of you."

"When did you first get to talk?"

"She got here a few days before the rest of you. She treats me like a person. One night I was scrubbing the dishes and she joined me, to help."

"That's very kind of her. No arguments or disputes between you two at all?"

"None."

"Okay," Scott pressed his hand to his forehead. "Is there anything else you feel would be helpful for us to know in our investigation?"

"Yeah, David is an asshole."

Scott stood up. "You're good to go on with your business now, Meredith." She walked out without another word.

Emily and Scott reviewed their notes and ideas together, trying to find something that would lead them to their killer. Alice was innocent. Her killer had to be a monster.

Emily glanced over at Scott, and a rush of gratitude washed over her. Their night together before Alice's body was found had forged an unshakeable bond. They had total trust in one another, having crossed each other off as suspects due to their ironclad alibis. This trust allowed them to work seamlessly as a team, their minds in sync as they pursued the truth.

Scott scratched his beard, thinking deeply about the investigation. "If you don't think it's David, we can look past him for now. But we can't rule him out completely, not without solid proof."

Emily began to sign, "I understand," she felt the pressure of accusing some of her oldest friends of *murder*—maybe it would be easier to assume one of the outsiders committed the crime. "I'm open to all of the possibilities, but there is something to be said about trusting your instincts."

As they continued to sift through their notes, Emily's hand brushed against something in her jacket pocket. Her confidence shifted when she pulled out Lily's diary, the small leather-bound book she had discovered earlier.

"Scott, look at this," she said, her voice barely above a whisper. "I found this diary when we were looking through the library. It belonged to a maid named Lily who worked here in the 1890s. I completely forgot about it until now."

Scott leaned in closer as Emily opened the diary with trembling hands. The faded pages held the thoughts of a young maid from 1893 and painted a vivid picture of life at the lodge over a century ago:

Aspen, Colorado – Spring, 1893

Today I learned of a girl named Mary. She was a maid who once worked at the lodge. They said she was young and pretty and looked like me. The other maids said not to talk about it. William lets me ask questions, but I am scared to ask about Mary. It took a long time, but he answers my questions now, too. He says it's dangerous to ask questions, but he wants to know the answers, too. William says Mary ran away, but I don't think she did. Maids don't run. Maids clean, and look proper, and look down when Mr. or Mrs. Belmont comes near. I don't think Mary ran away. I think something horrible happened to her.

I heard Mr. Belmont talking about hunting today. It didn't sound like he was talking about animals. This place scares me, and I don't want to be here anymore. But I worry what will happen if I try to leave. William tries to keep me calm. It is difficult to be calm. I think Mary tried to leave.

I talk to William a lot, and it is nice. He is the nicest person here, and he lets me cry to him. He held me when I cried, and he told me I was very beautiful. William makes me want to stay.

If you are here, leave. The lodge amplifies everything—twisting emotions until they break. It feeds on what's inside you, multiplying it tenfold. The joyful become ecstatic. The corrupt become monstrous. Get out while you still recognize yourself.

When Emily finished, she and Scott exchanged a look of shock and dismay. The implications of Lily's words hung heavy in the air between them.

"Emily," Scott said slowly, "if what Lily wrote is true, then this lodge has a history of bringing evil out in people."

Emily agreed, her mind racing. "And it seems like it wasn't just isolated incidents. The way Lily writes about Mary, about the danger of asking questions... It's like there was a systematic effort to silence and possibly harm these women."

Scott ran his fingers along the spines of nearby books. "Before we tell the others, maybe we should see what else we can find. They're already on edge—if we start talking about supernatural forces without more evidence, they'll think we're crazy."

Emily nodded and moved to search another shelf. Her hands trembled slightly as she pulled out a heavy leather-bound volume. "Look at this," she signed, laying the book on a nearby table. "It's a record of lodge employees from 1890 to 1895."

They bent over the yellowed pages together. Scott's finger traced down a column of neat handwriting until it stopped at a familiar name. "Here—Lily Anderson, hired January 1893." His finger moved down a few more lines. "And Mary Thompson... terminated December 1892. No reason given."

Emily's breath caught. She flipped back to Lily's diary, comparing dates. "Scott, Lily started working here just weeks after Mary disappeared. That can't be a coincidence."

"Keep looking," Scott urged. "There has to be more."

As they searched, Emily found herself drawn to a small collection of local newspapers, carefully preserved between the books. She spread them carefully on the table, mindful of their fragile state. A headline from 1892 caught her eye: "SEARCH FOR MISSING MAID ABANDONED."

The article was brief, noting only that the search for Mary Thompson, a maid at the prestigious Belmont Lodge, had been called off due to harsh winter conditions. The final line sent a chill down Emily's spine: "Miss Thompson is presumed to have left the area of her own accord."

"They didn't even look for her," Emily signed, her movements angry. "Just like Lily wrote—they wanted everyone to believe she ran away."

Scott placed a gentle hand on her shoulder. "Em, look at this." He held up another book, this one filled with photographs. On one page, a group of staff members posed stiffly before the lodge's entrance. The date at the bottom read "December 1892."

Emily leaned closer, studying the faces. In the back row, barely visible, stood a young woman with dark hair and solemn eyes. Below the photo, a neat hand had recorded the names of those pictured. The last one simply read "Mary T."

"She looks so young," Emily signed. "Not much older than we were in high school."

Scott closed the photo album carefully. "Emily, I think you're right—we need to tell the others what we've found. But we should be careful how we present it. They're already scared, and this..." He gestured to their research. "This could push them over the edge."

Emily considered this, then signed, "What if we focus on the emotional aspect first? The way the lodge affects people's feelings? That's something they might be able to relate to, especially after everything that's happened with Alice."

Scott nodded slowly. "Good thinking. We can gauge their reactions, see who's willing to listen. Then maybe we can share more about Lily and Mary if it seems right."

As they gathered their findings, Emily couldn't shake the feeling that they had just scratched the surface of a mystery far deeper and darker than they had initially imagined. The lodge's secrets were slowly unraveling, and she feared what other horrors they might uncover in their pursuit of the truth.

Night had fallen over the Belmont Lodge, bringing with it a silence that felt almost sacred. The group had gathered in the living room, none willing to sleep, all haunted by the image of Alice's body being carefully moved to the basement freezer. The fire crackled softly, its warmth doing little to chase away the bone-deep chill that had settled over them.

Emily sat curled in an armchair, watching the flames flutter. Her mind kept replaying the moment they had found Alice, trying to make sense of something that defied comprehension. Across the room, Brian hadn't moved from his position on the sofa for hours. His face was a mask of grief, eyes fixed on some distant point only he could see.

Claire paced near the window, her nervous energy a stark contrast to the room's stillness. Every few minutes, she would pause to peer out into the darkness, as if expecting to see something—or someone—moving in the shadows. David watched her from his position by the fireplace, his expression a complicated mix of concern and guilt.

"We should try to get some sleep," Scott suggested, his voice barely above a whisper. The words seemed to hang in the air, met with silence from the others.

Mark let out a bitter laugh. "Sleep? How are we supposed to sleep after—" He cut himself off, running a hand through his hair in frustration.

Emily noticed Brian flinch at Mark's words, his fingers twitching slightly as if reaching for his ever-present camera. But the camera sat untouched on the coffee table, its lens reflecting the firelight like a watching eye.

"Mark's right," Claire said, finally stopping her pacing. "I can't... I can't even think about sleeping. Not with Alice..." Her voice cracked on the name.

David stood, moving toward his wife, but Claire stepped away from his reaching hand. The rejection was subtle but clear. Emily watched as David's face fell, noting how he retreated to the bar cart instead, pouring himself a generous measure of whiskey.

"Does anyone want to talk about it?" Scott asked gently. "Sometimes it helps to—"

"Talk about how one of our best friends was murdered? About how we're trapped here with a killer?"

The word 'killer' seemed to echo through the room. Emily saw how it affected each person differently: Claire's quick intake of breath, David's tightening grip on his glass, Brian's barely perceptible tremor.

"We don't know that for certain," Emily signed, her movements catching everyone's attention. "The police will investigate when they get here. We shouldn't jump to conclusions."

Brian spoke for the first time in hours, his voice hoarse. "Emily's right. We can't... we can't think like that. Alice wouldn't want us to turn on each other."

Something in his tone made Emily's skin crawl, though she couldn't explain why. She watched as Brian finally reached for his camera, his movements almost reverent as he began scrolling through its display screen.

"I have so many pictures of her," he said softly. "From just these past few days. She was so beautiful. So alive." His voice caught on the last word.

Emily noticed how Brian's hands trembled slightly as he navigated through the pictures, how his breathing seemed to drag with each new image.

The grandfather clock in the hall struck, its chimes startling them all. Mark muttered something about needing air and disappeared into the kitchen. David, who had been unusually quiet, followed him.

"I should check on them," Scott signed to Emily before standing. She nodded, understanding his concern. They were all on edge, and Scott's steady presence might help prevent any conflicts from escalating.

Left alone with Brian and Claire, Emily felt the weight of unsaid words pressing down on her. Claire had moved away from Brian again, resuming her vigil by the window. Brian continued to scroll through his photos, though Emily noticed he had started the sequence over, watching Alice's last days play out in an endless repeat.

A loud crack from the fireplace made them all jump. Emily watched as a log split, sending sparks flying up the chimney. The flames cast strange shadows on the walls, making the room's corners seem deeper, darker.

"I keep expecting to wake up," Claire said suddenly, her voice small. "To find out this was all some horrible nightmare. That Alice will come bouncing down the stairs any minute, asking what's for breakfast."

Brian made a sound that might have been a laugh or a cry. "I know what you mean. It doesn't feel real."

Emily found herself reaching for the diary in her pocket, its presence somehow comforting. The lodge's history of tragedy seemed to press in around them, as if the walls themselves were absorbing their grief and reflecting it back amplified.

When Scott returned with Mark and David, the tension in the room had shifted into something heavier, more suffocating. They all resumed their positions—Claire by the window, David at the bar, Mark in his corner, Brian on the sofa with his camera, Emily in her chair, and Scott standing guard over them all.

None of them slept that night. They maintained their vigil until dawn, each lost in their own thoughts, their own guilt, their own fears. As the first gray light of morning began to seep through the windows, Emily couldn't shake the feeling that this night had changed them all in ways they had yet to understand.

The sun rose over the snow-covered mountains, but its light brought no warmth to the lodge. They had survived their first night without Alice, but Emily knew with crushing certainty that it was only the beginning. Whatever darkness had taken root in the Belmont Lodge, it was far from finished with them.

She glanced at Scott, finding comfort in his steady presence, then back at the others—her friends, now bound together by tragedy. As she watched Brian finally set down his camera, his movements careful and precise, a shiver ran down her spine. She couldn't explain it, but something about his grief felt... wrong. Like a photograph slightly out of focus, where everything appears normal at first glance but becomes increasingly unsettling the longer you look.

The day ahead loomed before them, full of questions without answers and shadows that seemed to grow deeper with each passing hour. They would face it together, but as Emily looked around at her friends' haunted faces, she wondered if any of them would emerge from this unchanged.

Or alive.

CHAPTER SIX—Tension

The group gathered in the living room, tension palpable in the air. Emily and Scott stood at the center, their faces grave as they prepared to share their findings from Lily's diary.

Emily's hands moved deliberately, "We've discovered something crucial about the lodge. It seems to have a way of amplifying people's internal thoughts and emotions."

Scott added, "It's as if the place is feeding off our fears and desires, making everything more intense."

Claire spoke up, her voice trembling slightly. "You know ... now that I think about it ..." She wrapped her arms around herself. "David, I think we fight every single time we stay here. Even that huge argument last Christmas about the wine glasses..." She trailed off, remembering. "Every time we visit, things get so intense between us."

David rolled his eyes. "Claire, please. We're all stressed and trapped here with a killer. Of course, emotions are running high." He stood up straighter, his tone matter-of-fact. "Let's not start inventing supernatural explanations for our marriage problems."

Emily signed, "Claire, I think you're right. The diary—it mentions voices that sang when Lily was happy. We think the lodge somehow taps into our psyche, making everything more intense."

Mark stood up abruptly, his face set in a hard mask. "That's all very interesting, but I think we're missing the point here. We need to focus on who killed Alice." His eyes narrowed when he turned to face David. "I think it's time we address the elephant in the room. You were downstairs that night. You had the easiest access out of all of us."

David's face paled. "What? You can't be serious. I would never—"

Before anyone could react, Mark pulled out a pocket knife, the blade glinting in the dim light of the room. "I'm done playing games. We need answers, and we need them now."

The room erupted into chaos. Scott stepped over across the room to position himself between Mark and David. Claire let out a strangled cry.

"Mark, put the knife down," Emily signed frantically. "This isn't helping anyone."

For a tense moment, Mark stood frozen with the knife still in his hand. Then, slowly, he lowered it, his face a mix of confusion and shame. "I ... I don't trust David. We just—we need to find the killer before anyone else is killed."

Mark stormed out while the others remained in the living room, still shaken by his outburst. Emily wandered off herself and found the game room door cracked open. She wasn't surprised to find Mark there. He sat staring blankly at a chessboard.

"We need to talk," she signed as she approached him.

Mark looked up with haunted eyes. "I know. I'm sorry about earlier, okay? I wasn't going to hurt him or anything, I just—I don't want to be here anymore."

Emily sat down across from him, her gaze steady. "It's not just about today, Mark. You've always had anger issues. In school, you were always getting into fights. It seems like you're still that bruised-up little kid who needs a little self-control."

Mark's face twisted. "You don't understand. It wasn't just at school. You don't know what home was like for me and Claire. Our father..." He bit his nail mid-sentence. "He was an alcoholic. Every night at home, if the dishes stacked too high, or the Jazz lost, I was getting hit. That was my life every single night. Not everyone had a great dad like you."

"I didn't know." Emily's expression softened slightly, but she remained firm. "I'm sorry you went through that, Mark. You could have reached out to one of us for support." She positioned herself closer to him. "You need to take care of yourself."

"I know." Mark's tone switched, gentler now. "I've been trying to get better. I really have. And I need to apologize for what happened in high school. Cheating on you... it was the biggest mistake of my life."

Emily watched him carefully, trying to gauge his sincerity. "Mark, why are you telling me this now? What is the point? That was ten years ago."

Mark took a deep breath. "Because I love you, Emily. I never stopped loving you. I want another chance. I feel like I've changed, and I think we could be happy together."

Emily felt a pang in her chest, a mix of old pain and new understanding. But when she spoke, her signs were clear and confident. "Mark, I appreciate your honesty. But this is inappropriate given our current circumstances. We're dealing with a murderer, for heaven's sake." She shook her head and inched away from him.

She paused to gather her thoughts. "Besides, regardless of your feelings, I need to be clear about something. Scott and I... care about each other. When we get out of this lodge, I plan to move forward with him, not step back in time with you."

Mark's face fell, and something cold settled in his stomach. Ten years, and she was choosing Scott? The thought of the straight-laced officer made his jaw clench, but he forced himself to maintain his composure. This wasn't how he'd imagined this conversation going.

Emily continued, "I'm willing to give you another chance at friendship. I'll admit I've been holding some things against you from high school, and I'm open to setting those aside. We've all grown and changed since then."

"Friendship," Mark repeated, his voice hollow. He swallowed hard, fighting back the bitterness threatening to surface. "I guess that's better than nothing." His fingers curled slightly at his sides, but he kept his tone even. "I just... I never pictured you with someone so... bland."

Emily's eyes hardened. "Don't start. You don't have the right to have any opinion about my dating life."

"I didn't mean..." Mark started, then stopped himself. Every instinct screamed to point out how mundane Scott was, how beneath her, but he bit it back. "I just want you to be with someone who actually knows how to make you happy."

"This right here?" Emily gestured between them, her voice steady but keen. "This is exactly why friendship is all I can offer. Scott may play by the rules, but at least he has integrity. He knows who he is. And for the record? I made up my mind about him – I love him."

The word 'love' hit Mark like a bullet. He struggled to keep his expression neutral even as his stomach churned. *She couldn't be serious. Scott? The most boring man in the world?* He forced himself to nod, though the movement felt mechanical.

"I don't need your approval, Mark. Or your permission." Emily straightened her spine, looking more certain with every word. "Scott makes me feel safe. Respected. Valued."

The words stung more than Mark wanted to admit. He wanted to argue, to point out how pathetically predictable her choice was, but he knew it would only push her further away. Instead, he managed a tight smile. "If that's really what you want."

Emily reached out and touched his hand gently. "I don't think you're a bad person, Mark. And right now with everything that's happening, we all need friends we can trust. I need you to be that."

Mark spoke softly, pushing down his disgust at the situation. "You're right. And I am truly sorry for everything. Not just for cheating, but for all the pain I've caused you."

"I want to believe you," Emily signed. "Actions speak louder than words. You need to control your anger. I'm still figuring out the weird things going on in the lodge. The best thing you can do for our relationship right now is show me that you aren't a killer." She stared concerningly at him.

The lodge's influence hung over them like a dark cloud, and Emily knew that until they solved the mystery of Alice's death, no one was above suspicion—not even Mark.

"Let's get back to the others," Emily signed finally. "There's more important things we need to focus on."

Mark sniffled and stood up, his thoughts a turbulent mix of regret and resentment. When they left the game room, Emily felt they had taken a small step forward. As they entered the lobby of the lodge, Emily spotted Scott standing by the window, gazing out at the snow. She approached him, and they embraced.

"The snow is getting worse," Scott said concernedly. "We need it to melt, but it's probably piled up three, maybe four feet since yesterday."

Emily pulled back, her hands moving as she signed, "Have you checked with David or Claire if there's any roof access?"

Scott shook his head. "David and I went up to the roof hatch. There must be a thousand pounds of snow weighing it down." He sighed and scratched his head. "At this point, I just keep checking to see if the snow will melt or if the phone lines will get fixed. We're lucky that the power is still on."

"You think we'll lose power soon?"

"Oh, it's a matter of time. That's why I'm so adamant about finding a way out."

Emily nodded. Her eyes drifted to the window. The endless expanse of white outside seemed to mock their predicament. This prison held them captive with a killer.

Just then, a panicked yell shattered the tense silence.

"Help! Someone, help us!" David's voice echoed through the lodge, tinged with terror.

"We're in the basement stairwell!" Brian's shout followed, equally frantic.

Scott tugged at Emily's arm before rushing towards the source of the cries. They thundered down the stairs, hearts pounding in their chests. As they reached the basement level, they saw David and Brian, frozen in shock, standing at the foot of the stairs.

And then they saw her.

Meredith hung from the ceiling, suspended by a crude noose. Her lifeless eyes stared blankly ahead. Her body swayed gently in the stale basement air.

CHAPTER SEVEN—Guilty

The grandfather clock in the lobby chimed midnight. Its solemn tones echoed through the silent halls of Belmont Lodge. The group huddled on the narrow basement stairs, their breath visible in the frigid air. Despite the roaring fireplace upstairs, the cold had seeped into every corner of the lodge. It was as if the snow outside had found its way in to chill them to their very bones.

Emily stood near the bottom of the stairs, her eyes fixed on Meredith's lifeless form swinging gently from the doorframe. On the nearby table lay a note written in that same distinctive crimson ink they'd seen before - a single word that seemed to mock them: "GUILTY." Emily felt a tight knot of dread that made each breath a struggle.

Mark was the first to move. His face was stunned in the dim light. "We need to get her down," he said, his voice hoarse with shock. He pulled out the knife he had concealed earlier, the same one that had caused such tension in the group just hours before. Now, it served a new purpose.

"Brian, David, can you support her?" Scott asked, taking charge of the situation. The two men moved forward with hesitation. They grasped Meredith's legs to support her weight and relieve the pressure on her neck. Emily could see their hands shaking and their faces contorted with revulsion and sorrow.

Mark reached up, and his hand trembled visibly while he cut the rope where it was tied to the doorframe. The knife rasped as it cut through the fibers. Each scrape of the blade sent a shudder through the group.

"Careful!" Claire exclaimed, her warning unnecessary. "Don't let her fall."

When the last fibers gave way, Meredith's body slumped with a thud into Brian and David's arms. They staggered slightly under the sudden weight but managed to keep their footing.

"Over here," Scott directed, indicating a clear space on the cold concrete floor. Slowly, reverently, they lowered Meredith's body to the ground. Emily couldn't tear her eyes away from Meredith's peaceful face, nor from that damning note on the table. Was she really that wicked? How could someone who'd seemed so normal harbor such darkness?

Claire turned away to retch violently. David rushed to her side and held her hair back while she emptied her stomach onto the hardwood floor.

Emily swallowed hard, trying to keep her stomach contents down. The cold of the basement seemed to intensify and seep into her bones. She wrapped her arms around herself, but it did little to ward off the chill.

Mark grabbed the back of his neck, his face a mask of shock and disbelief. "She must have been overwhelmed with guilt." His voice shook. "Guilt over killing Alice... It drove her to this."

The reality of what they saw settled over the group like a heavy blanket. Meredith, consumed by guilt, had taken her own life after confessing to Alice's murder. The silence that followed was broken by Claire's continued sobs and the sound of dripping water in the dark recesses of the basement.

Emily's mind raced, trying to process the scene before her. Meredith's body looked small and fragile on the cold concrete floor. Her skin was pale, almost translucent in the dim light, and her lips had taken on a bluish tinge. Despite the horror of the situation, Emily couldn't help but notice how peaceful Meredith's face looked. In death, it was as though she had found a release from torment.

The group stood frozen, each lost in their thoughts. Brian leaned against the wall, his eyes closed and his breathing shallow. Mark paced. Scott remained kneeling by Meredith's body, his medical training seemingly at war with his emotional response to the situation.

The realization of their complete isolation hit Emily anew. They were trapped here, cut off from the outside world, with *two* dead bodies. The walls seemed to close in around them.

"I'm cold," Claire said hoarsely. "David, honey, it's getting too cold in here."

Taking a deep breath, Emily signed, "Let's move to the living room. We need to talk about this, figure out our next steps." Her hands shook slightly as she formed the words, but her stare was steady, focused.

The others nodded, grateful for any direction in this chaos. Slowly, reluctantly, they made their way back up the stairs, leaving Meredith's body behind. Emily was the last to leave, casting one final glance at the scene. The image of Meredith's body, with that damning note, was seared into her memory. She knew it would haunt her dreams for years to come.

When they emerged from the basement, the relative warmth of the main floor washed over them, but it did little to dispel the chill that had settled in their hearts. They entered the living room where the fire still crackled in the hearth. It was a mockery of warmth and comfort in the face of their reality.

The group gathered in the living room, drawn to the flickering warmth of the fireplace like moths to a flame. The crackling of burning logs filled the silence. Emily sank into a plush armchair. She watched as David guided Claire to the sofa with his arm protectively around her shoulders.

Claire's eyes looked lost and red-rimmed from crying. David lowered her gently onto the cushions before heading to the bar cart in the corner. He returned moments later with a glass of water, which Claire accepted with trembling hands. As she sipped, David sat beside her. His hand moved in soothing circles on her back.

The others found their places around the room. Brian slumped into a chair, his sights fixed on the flames. Mark paced back and forth behind the sofa. Meanwhile, Scott leaned against the mantle, his fingers tapping in thought.

For several long minutes, no one spoke. The only sounds were the crackling fire, Claire's occasional sniffles, and the howling wind outside. The storm seemed to mirror their inner turmoil, its fury matching the tumultuous emotions that churned within each of them.

Finally, Mark broke the silence. "So ... I guess that's it then." His voice was unnaturally loud in the quiet room.

There were nods of agreement from around the room. David's hand stilled on Claire's back when he looked up. "It makes sense," he said slowly. "The guilt must have been eating her alive. She couldn't live with what she'd done."

"But why?" Claire's voice was barely above a whisper. "Why would Meredith kill Alice?"

"Who knows?" David replied.

Claire demanded, "David, we need to get out of here. Smash a window or something I don't care."

"I know. We'll give it one more day, I really think the snow is going to let up soon, we just have to make it through the night."

Emily's mind raced as she listened to the others discuss the apparent ending of their nightmare. Something didn't sit right with her. She remembered her conversation with Alice on that first day at the lodge, how Alice had mentioned Meredith with fondness in her voice.

How could someone speak so warmly of a friend one day and be murdered by them the next? What could have happened to drive Meredith to such a desperate act? And why wait days before confessing and taking her own life?

As the others continued to talk, seemingly satisfied with their conclusion, Emily was unable to shake her doubts. She watched her friends and noted the relief that seemed to wash over them now that they believed the mystery was solved. But for Emily, the questions only multiplied.

"I can't believe it's all over," David said, running a hand through his hair.

Scott agreed. "I know what you mean. But sometimes the truth is simpler than we expect. Meredith must have snapped, killed Alice, and then couldn't live with the guilt."

"Did she seem suspicious when you guys interviewed her yesterday?" Mark asked.

Scott shook his head, staring at the floor. "Not really, but you know some people are better at hiding things than others."

Emily wanted to speak up, to voice her doubts about this conclusion, but something held her back. Perhaps it was the look of relief on her friends' faces, the way the tension seemed to be draining from the room. Who was she to take that peace away from them?

While she wrestled with her thoughts, Mark immediately stopped his pacing. "Listen," he said hesitantly, "I know this isn't the best time, but ... we need to talk about something."

All eyes turned to him, curiosity mingling with weariness on their faces.

"I, uh ..." Mark started. He glanced around the room, clearly struggling to find the right words. "I don't mean to be insensitive, but ... we need to address the fact that Alice's body is starting to smell."

Claire's eyes narrowed. "How dare you, Mark? What could possibly be more important right now?"

Mark held up his hands defensively. "Hey I'm not trying to be insensitive, but—"

Scott cut him off, his voice firm but understanding. "No. Mark's right. We shouldn't be sharing a space with a dead body, especially not when it's our friend." He paused, twiddling his thumbs for a second. "I think I saw a meat freezer down in the basement. Is that right, David?"

David nodded slowly, his face pale. "Yeah, there is. It's pretty big ... We could fit the—um, the bodies down there."

A heavy silence fell over the room as the implications of David's words sank in. Emily felt her stomach churn at the thought of what they were considering.

Scott took a deep breath before continuing. "Okay, here's what we'll do. We'll move them to the freezer and leave them there until the snow melts and the police can look at both of them." He met each person's eyes. "I know this sounds horrible, but listen. Under most normal circumstances, you should never, ever move a dead body from its initial location. But we're trapped in here, and we need to make this lodge as livable as possible. We don't know how much longer we'll be stuck here."

Claire's face crumpled, fresh tears spilling down her cheeks. "This can't be happening," she whispered.

"Claire, Emily," Scott said gently, "you two stay up here. We'll move Meredith first."

Emily wanted to protest, to insist on helping, but the words caught in her throat. She watched as Scott, Mark, Brian, and David stood up, their faces set in an uncomfortable stiffness.

While the men left the room to carry out their task, Emily sat frozen. The crackling of the fire seemed too cheerful, too normal for the horror of their situation. She glanced at Claire who sat with her arms wrapped tightly around herself, staring blankly at the floor.

Emily felt the vibration from footsteps on the stairs, and then nothing. Her mind raced, imagining what was happening in the basement. She got up and moved across the sectional to Claire.

"Here." Emily wrapped a blanket around the two of them, and Claire's head sunk into Emily's chest in complete surrender.

Minutes stretched into what felt like hours. Emily was unable to hear any sound from below, both dreading and needing to know what was happening. When the men finally returned, their faces were pale and their movements slow and heavy.

"It's done," Scott said simply, collapsing into an armchair. "We'll move Alice in a bit. We just ... We need a moment."

The room fell into silence once more with each person lost in their thoughts. Emily's mind whirled with questions and doubts. Despite the apparent confession written on the notecard, something about this whole situation felt off. How could things have gone so wrong so quickly?

When she saw the shock and grief etched on their faces, Emily knew this experience would continue to haunt them for years to come. But beneath her sorrow, determination grew. She needed to get to the bottom of this, no matter what it took.

"Claire," Emily began to ask, "I realized with Meredith gone, we'll have to go through the food in the house and make sure we have enough to ration for everyone."

Claire sat up, moving slowly "There's plenty of food in the pantry downstairs. Water bottles too." She rubbed her eyes. "I *do* know how to cook, you know." She revealed the slightest smile.

Emily defended, "No, I'm sure—I just meant—"

Claire nodded. "It was nice having Meredith take care of all those things, especially this past weekend so I could spend more time with you all."

The two of them reflected on the past few days and the horror of it all.

The grandfather clock in the hall chimed another hour, the sound eerily familiar. Outside, the storm continued to rage, growing stronger by the minute.

CHAPTER EIGHT—Doubts

Dawn crept through the frost-laden windows of the Belmont Lodge, casting long shadows across the worn hardwood floors.

Emily stirred from a fitful sleep. The events of the previous night still clouded her mind. The clock on her nightstand read 7:15 a.m., but time seemed to have lost all meaning in this isolated haven of snow and secrets.

As Emily made her way downstairs, the scent of freshly brewed coffee and sizzling bacon wafted through the air. In the kitchen, she found Claire busying herself at the stove, spatula in hand, a look of forced normalcy on her face.

"Good morning," Claire said with an overly cheerful demeanor. "I thought we could all use a hearty breakfast. How do you like your eggs?"

Emily signed back, "Scrambled, please," before sitting at the kitchen island. She watched as Claire moved about the kitchen. Her actions were mechanical as though cooking breakfast could somehow restore order to the group's shattered dynamic.

One by one, the others trickled into the kitchen, drawn by the promise of food and the illusion of routine. Scott, his hair disheveled and dark circles under his eyes, gave Emily a weak smile as he poured himself a large mug of coffee. Mark slouched into a chair while Claire set plates around the table, the ceramic clinking against wood like a metronome.

"Thanks," Brian mumbled when Claire placed a plate in front of him. Emily watched as he picked up his fork, then set it down again, his fingers tracing absent patterns on the tablecloth. The gesture was so familiar—Alice used to do the same thing when she was lost in thought. Five years of sharing meals together, and now her place at the table sat empty, a void as tangible as the meat freezer where her body lay.

Steam rose from Emily's coffee as she studied the faces around her, each lost in their own version of grief. The others seemed to find comfort in answers, in having someone to blame. It was easier that way—to package tragedy into something neat and digestible. But Emily had spent too many late nights reading over case files not to recognize when something felt wrong. The detective in her couldn't rest, even as her friends eagerly embraced closure.

Emily couldn't accept what everyone else had. Meredith killed Alice? It felt sloppy. The group was desperate for answers, and just when chaos broke out, the solution conveniently presented itself. The supposed killer revealed herself in front of everyone and then promptly ended her own life before anyone could question her further.

After breakfast, the others dispersed to various parts of the lodge. Emily caught Scott's arm gently. "Can we talk?" she signed. "Privately?"

Scott got up, his posture shifting slightly at the serious look on Emily's face. "Of course. Let's go to the library."

A large desk dominated one corner while a pair of leather armchairs sat before a cold fireplace. After they entered, Scott closed the door behind them.

"What's on your mind, Emily?" Scott asked concernedly.

Emily took a deep breath, her hands moving decisively as she signed. "I don't think it's over, Scott. I think there's more to this story than we're seeing."

Scott's face clouded with worry, but he gestured for Emily to continue.

Emily reached into her pocket and pulled out the blackmail note they had found earlier. She laid it on the desk beside the suicide note, her hands trembling slightly as she pulled out a magnifying glass from the drawer. "Look at this," she signed, gesturing for Scott to come closer.

Scott leaned in, his brow furrowed. "What am I looking for?"

"The letters," Emily signed, her movements precise and controlled. "Look at how Meredith wrote 'GUILTY.' Compare it to the letters in this note - especially the 'G' and 'T.' They're... different."

Scott studied both notes carefully, his medical training making him naturally analytical. After a moment, he nodded slowly. "There are some slight variations, yes. But Emily, handwriting can change dramatically under emotional distress. If she wrote this right before..." He trailed off, unwilling to finish the thought.

Emily wasn't satisfied. Her hands moved faster now, her signs becoming more emphatic. "But what about this - I watched her cooking dinner when we first got here. She was cutting potatoes with her left hand. Meredith was left-handed, Scott. So why was the pen found on the right side of the note?"

Scott scratched his head, looking uncomfortable. "Emily, honey, I understand you're upset. We all are. But sometimes... sometimes things aren't as complicated as we want them to be. Sometimes the simplest explanation is the right one."

"The simplest explanation isn't always the truth," Emily signed. "These details matter."

"They're interesting observations," Scott conceded, his voice gentle. "But they're not enough to... what are you suggesting, exactly?"

Emily's hands fell to her sides. How could she explain the nagging feeling in her gut? The sense that they were all missing something important? But looking at Scott's face - the grief, exhaustion, and gentle concern - she knew she wouldn't convince him. Not now, anyway.

"Maybe you're right," she signed finally, but her eyes lingered on the two notes, studying the subtle differences in the letters that seemed to mock her with their secrets.

Scott reached out, gently taking Emily's hands in his own. "I know you want answers, Em. We all do. But we're all exhausted, stressed, and traumatized. Maybe we need to take a step back, try to process everything that's happened."

Emily pulled her hands away. Her eyes flashed with calculation. "I can't just let this go, Scott. Something isn't right here, and I'm going to figure out what it is."

Scott sighed, his shoulders slumping slightly. "I'm worried about you. I don't want you getting hurt or ... or worse. Please just promise me you'll be careful."

Emily's expression softened at the concern in Scott's eyes. She nodded, signing, "I'll be careful."

When they left the study, Emily's mind was already racing with plans. She knew she would have to be discreet, to alarm the others or tip off anyone who might be involved.

Scott watched her go with a mixture of love, admiration, and worry etched on his face. He wanted to believe that the nightmare was over, that they could all start to heal and move on. But a small part of him, the part that had fallen in love with Emily's brilliant mind and dedicated observation, couldn't help but wonder if she might be right after all.

As the day wore on, Emily grew restless, and her mind churned with theories and questions. The others seemed content to accept Meredith's guilt, but Emily couldn't shake the feeling that they were missing something crucial. She decided to investigate on her own, starting with a more careful observation of her friends' behaviors.

As Emily made her way through the lodge, her keen eyes took in every detail. She noticed David inside the game room absently rolling pool balls across the table. She paused before stepping into the room.

"Mind if I join you?" Emily signed, catching David's attention.

David looked up. A flicker of unease crossed his face before he shrugged his shoulders. "Sure," he said. He reached for a cue stick to hand to her.

Emily took the cue, chalked the tip, and watched David set up the balls. His movements lacked his usual precision. As they began to play, Emily carefully crafted her approach.

"Nice shot," she signed after David sank a ball, though it had just barely crawled into the pocket. His aim was off. Significantly.

David mumbled his thanks. His eyes moved around the room. Nervous energy radiated off him.

Emily rested the pool stick on the edge of the table, "You know, I've been thinking about Alice." She paused to gauge David's reaction. "Trying to remember our last interactions with her."

David's hand tightened on his cue stick. "I get that," he said, his voice slightly strained.

Emily nodded, sinking a ball into the corner pocket with a satisfying clunk. "Yeah. I remembered seeing you two on the ski lift that day. You seemed to be having a pleasant conversation."

David's head tilted slightly as he tried to remember. He forced a smile. "Ah, yes. Alice was always fun to talk to."

Emily straightened up, her eyes locking onto David's. "What I remember specifically is how *light* the conversation seemed at first. You were both laughing, everything appeared normal. But when Alice got off the lift, she was visibly upset about something. Her whole demeanor had changed in those few minutes. What did you two talk about, David?"

David's cue stick slipped, sending the white ball careening off course. He stared at Emily for a long moment. Finally, he sighed and set the cue stick aside.

"You're right," he admitted, his voice low. "We had a conversation, and it upset Alice."

Emily waited, her look steady, encouraging him to continue.

David waved a hand over his mouth and yawned, looking suddenly tired. "Alice ... She confided in me about something personal. Something she was struggling with."

"What was it?" Emily pressed gently.

David hesitated and then whispered, "She told me she was thinking about *leaving* Brian. She said she felt trapped, that their relationship wasn't all she thought it would be. She felt like she had lost her freedom and wanted to take it back."

Emily's eyebrows rose. This was news to her.

"At first, we were just talking about it casually," David continued. "But then ... then I made a mistake. I told her that maybe she was right, that maybe she and I could try and— and you know, be *together*."

"Why would you say that?" Emily asked, her stare concerning.

David looked away. "Because ... I felt lonely, Emily. I know it sounds wrong, but ... I couldn't help it. When Alice told me she was having doubts—I don't know—I guess a small part of me saw an opportunity."

Emily's mind reeled with this new information. "So when she got off the lift ..."

"She was angry with me," David finished. "She accused me of trying to manipulate her, of taking advantage of her vulnerability. She was right, of course. I immediately regretted what I'd said, but the damage was done."

Emily stared at David, processing this revelation. "Does Claire know about this?"

David shook his head, and a bitter laugh escaped. "No, but it's complicated. It's not even that I had any feelings for Alice, more of a lack of feelings for *Claire*. The truth is, after this reunion, I was planning to give Claire divorce papers."

Emily fell completely speechless.

David continued, his voice heavy with emotion. "I know you all just see what's on social media, and everything looks perfect, but neither of us has been happy for a long time. I just don't think it's going to work out anymore."

As David was mid-explanation, movement in the doorway caught Emily's eye. She looked up to see Claire standing behind him, her face consumed with shock and hurt.

"This is the first I've heard of this," Claire said, her voice barely above a whisper.

David whirled around. His face drained of color when he saw his wife. "Claire, I—"

Emily quickly moved toward the door, feeling like an intruder in a deeply personal moment. "I should go," she signed, looking between David and Claire.

As Emily slipped out of the game room, she could see the beginnings of what promised to be an intense conversation. Her mind whirled with all she had learned.

The revelation about David's feelings for Alice and his plans to divorce Claire added a new layer to the relationships within their group.

For a moment, they stood in silence, the weight of David's revelation hanging heavily between them.

Claire was the first to break the silence. Her voice trembled with anger and hurt. "Divorce papers? You were waiting for a proper opportunity to tell me you want a *divorce*?"

David let out a deep sigh. His face was a mask of guilt and resignation. "Claire, I ... I'm sorry. Obviously, I didn't mean for it to come out like this."

"How exactly did you want it to come out, David?" Claire's voice rose, her composure cracking. "Were you going to wait until all our friends left, then casually mention over dinner that you want to end our marriage?"

David took a step towards her, but Claire held up a hand. "Don't. Just ... don't come near me right now."

He stepped back. "I know this is a shock, Claire. I've been struggling with how to tell you for months."

"Months?" Claire's jaw dropped in disbelief. "You've been planning this for months?"

David's shoulders slumped. "I didn't want to ruin the reunion. I thought ... I thought it would be better to wait, to give us one last good memory together before ..."

"Before you shattered everything?" Claire finished bitterly.

"That's not fair," David said, a hint of frustration creeping into his tone. "Our marriage has been struggling for years. You know that as well as I do."

Claire laughed humorlessly. "Oh, so now it's my fault too? Is that why you were cozying up to Alice on the ski lift?"

David's face paled. "I wasn't going to do anything, I don't think—I just—"

"How dare you? You didn't want to talk to me about how you were feeling, so you went and found one of my oldest friends to pull a move on?"

David sighed heavily. "Alice and I ... It's not what you think. We were just talking."

"About what?" Claire demanded.

"About her relationship with Brian. About ... About feelings." David's voice was barely above a whisper.

Claire's eyes narrowed. "Feelings? What kind of feelings?"

David met her gaze with an expression of guilt and defiance. "She wanted *out* of her relationship, Claire. Okay? I'm trying to keep my voice down out of consideration for her grieving boyfriend, but she wanted to leave him. I didn't mean to talk to Alice about these things, but I guess I just related to what she was telling me, and that feeling took over."

The sound of Claire's hand connecting with David's cheek echoed. David stumbled back, more from shock than the force of the blow.

"How dare you?" Claire hissed. Tears flowed freely down her cheeks. "How dare you throw away our marriage for *nothing* and then go on and tell everyone else about it except me?"

David touched his cheek and winced. "It's not *nothing*, Claire. Our marriage has been over for a long time; we've just been too afraid to admit it."

Claire shook her head, her anger giving way to a deep, aching sadness. "I thought we were happy. I thought ... I thought we were working through our issues."

"You think so?" David asked softly. "Or were we just going through the motions? When was the last time we talked, Claire? Really connected?"

Claire was silent for a long moment, her mind racing through memories of their life together. "I ... I don't know," she finally admitted.

David nodded, and a sad smile on his face. "That's been our problem. We've been living parallel lives, not a shared one. I care about you. I always will. But I'm not in love with you anymore. And I don't think you're in love with me either."

Claire sank into a nearby chair, the fight draining out of her. "There are counselors for these kinds of issues. Books. When something isn't working, you don't just give up. You've really made up your mind?"

David knelt in front of her and was careful not to touch her. "I think it's for the best. For both of us. We deserve a chance at real happiness, even if it's not with each other."

Claire looked at him—really looked at him—for what felt like the first time in years. She saw the weariness in his eyes, the weight of unhappiness that had been dragging him down. And she realized with a start that she recognized that same weight in herself.

"What about Alice?" she asked hoarsely.

David shook his head. "Alice was ... a wake-up call. A signal to myself that I could still feel something. But she's not the reason for this. This is about us, Claire. About what we've become and what we're not anymore."

Claire nodded slowly, her anger giving way to a numb acceptance. "I think ... I think I need some time alone, David. To process all of this."

David stood up, respecting her wish. "Of course. Take all the time you need. I'll be here when you're ready to talk more."

As David turned to leave, Claire's voice stopped him. "David?"

He looked back at her.

"Sleep in the library."

David's eyes hardened with annoyance and a deeply rooted pain. "I was planning on it."

With that, he left the room, leaving Claire alone with her thoughts and the shattered remnants of what she had believed to be a happy marriage.

As the door closed behind David, Claire allowed herself to break down. Her sobs echoed in the empty game room. Outside, the storm continued to rage, a fitting backdrop to the emotional tempest that had just unfolded.

As Emily returned to her room, she knew she had stumbled onto something significant. The comfortable narrative the others had settled into was far from the whole story.

When she pushed open her bedroom door, she was surprised to find Scott inside, folding clothes from a laundry basket on the bed.

Scott looked up as she entered, a warm smile on his face. "Hey, I hope you don't mind. I thought I'd do our laundry while I had the chance."

Emily's eyebrows rose. "Oh, no of course. That's so thoughtful. Thank you," she signed, moving closer to the bed.

As she approached, she noticed Scott was folding a pair of her underwear. A slight flush crept up her cheeks, for she realized he had been handling her *delicates*. Scott, noticing her expression, quickly set the garment aside.

"Sorry," he signed, looking a bit embarrassed himself. "I didn't mean to make you uncomfortable."

Emily shook her head, a small smile tugging at her lips. "It's okay," she signed back. " ... Maybe a *little* intimate, I guess."

They looked at each other for a moment before they broke into soft laughter, and the awkwardness dissipated. Emily leaned in and placed a gentle kiss on Scott's cheek. She was grateful for his thoughtfulness and the moment of normalcy in all the chaos.

"I'm going to look over my notes for a bit," Emily signed, moving to the other side of the bed.

Scott smiled and returned to his folding. "Let me know if you need any help," he offered.

Emily grabbed her notepad from the desk and settled onto the bed, flipping through the pages of interview notes she had collected. Her eyes scanned the words, desperate for anything out of the ordinary, any detail she might have missed.

She returned to the notes from Meredith's interview, reading them over and over. Something about it kept nagging at her, but she couldn't quite put her finger on what it was. The lack of a clear motive for Meredith to harm Alice was particularly troubling.

Maybe I just didn't know *their relationship well enough to even assume motive*, Emily thought to herself, chewing on her lower lip. She had always seen Alice and Meredith as friends, but now she wondered how much of that friendship had been genuine and how much had been a facade.

Emily's mind raced with possibilities. Could there have been some hidden rivalry between them? Some secret that Meredith had discovered about Alice? Or was she looking at this all wrong? Maybe Meredith wasn't the killer at all, despite the apparent confession.

She was so absorbed in her thoughts that she barely noticed Scott finishing the laundry and settling into a chair with a book. The room was quiet except for the occasional rustle of pages and the scratch of Emily's pen as she jotted down new theories.

Just as Emily thought she might be onto something with a new connection forming in her mind, the room plunged into darkness. The abrupt loss of light startled her, causing her to drop her pen.

She felt movement on the bed, and then Scott's hand found hers, giving it a reassuring squeeze. As her eyes adjusted to the darkness, she could make out his silhouette.

"I think the power's out," Scott signed, his hands barely visible in the dim moonlight filtering through the curtains.

CHAPTER NINE—Dark

Glenwood, Utah – 2001

The soft glow of the table lamp illuminated the cozy living room. Five-year-old Emily sat cross-legged on the couch in a matching pajama set, her brow furrowed in concentration. Her father, Michael, sat beside her, his eyes twinkling with amusement as he watched his daughter ponder her next move in their game of Clue.

Emily's small hands moved decisively as she signed, "Is it *Colonel Mustard* ...in the *study* ... with the *wrench*?"

Michael chuckled and laid Colonel Mustard's card down on the table, shaking his head in laughter. Emily's face fell in her hands, her frustration evident.

"That is not funny, Dad!" she signed, her lower lip pouting.

Michael gently patted her on the back. His hands moved in a soothing rhythm as he signed, "If you're stuck, then you know you have to keep going. The answer is there; you just have to find it."

Emily let out a groan, but her father's words seemed to renew her will power. They continued taking turns, Emily's eyes darting between the board and her cards, searching for the elusive solution.

As the game drew to a close, Emily suddenly grinned and signed, "Okay, I have my guess!"

He chuckled and signed back, "Go ahead, honey."

Her hands moved excitedly as she signed, "It's *Mr. Green* with the *wrench* in the *library*!"

He shrugged his shoulders and signed, "I don't have any of those."

She took out the three cards from their sleeve and it was exactly as she had guessed.

"I win! I win!" she signed, bouncing with excitement, her smile stretching from ear to ear.

Emily took his hand and allowed herself to be led to her bedroom. She climbed into bed. Meanwhile, Michael positioned himself beside her, and his hands wove a bedtime story in the air between them. Emily watched, transfixed, as the tale unfolded. Her father's expressions and gestures brought the characters to life.

There was something special about stories of princesses and a knight in shining armor, especially the way he made them come to life. Her father knew exactly what she wanted to dream about.

After the story ended, Michael leaned down and kissed Emily's forehead. She snuggled deeper under the covers, her eyes already heavy with sleep. Just before Michael left the room, Emily signed a quick reminder, "Leave the door cracked open, please."

Michael nodded. To a child whose entire world was often shrouded in silence, the addition of darkness could be incredibly isolating. The absence of sound and light meant a complete disconnection from the world around her.

Michael left the door slightly ajar to allow a sliver of light to penetrate the darkness. Emily's fear of the dark would likely follow her into adulthood. But he also understood that with love, support, and the resilience he saw in her, she would learn to face her fears head-on.

In the years to come, Emily would draw strength from moments like these—the comfort of her father's presence, the encouragement to persevere, and the profound understanding that her fear of the dark was not a mere childhood phobia, but an overwhelming isolation of sensory loss.

Aspen, Colorado – Present Day

Emily's heart pounded as the darkness engulfed her, the sudden loss of power plunging the room into an inky blackness. She felt paralyzed, her childhood fear of the dark rushing back in an overwhelming wave.

Beside her, Scott fumbled in his pockets. A moment later, a small flame flickered to life from a cigarette lighter, casting an eerie glow across his face. He turned to Emily, and his free hand moved in a quick, reassuring sign.

"Here," he signed and placed the lighter in her hand. "Hold onto this. I'll find my flashlight."

Emily grasped it, her fingers curling around the warm metal of the lighter. She focused on the small flame and tried to steady her breathing to calm her racing heart. She noted her surroundings. The shadows on the walls. The dim light that only seemed to emphasize the vastness of the darkness surrounding them.

The pounding of footsteps reverberated in the hallway, and a moment later, the other members of the group appeared in the doorway. Their faces were pale and drawn in the flickering light. Claire stood apart from David, her arms wrapped tightly around herself as if seeking comfort. Mark and Brian hovered uncertainly, and their eyes darted around the room.

"The power's out in the whole lodge," David said, strained. "And the storm's only getting worse."

Scott reappeared with a flashlight in hand. He swept the beam around the room. The harsh white light cut through the darkness. "We need to conserve our resources," he said firmly. "Flashlights, batteries, food, water ... We don't know how long this outage will last."

Emily's mind already raced with the implications. With the power out and the storm raging outside, their isolation was even more acute. They were cut off from the outside world, trapped in a lodge with a killer still on the loose and with dwindling resources.

Claire's voice trembled when she asked, "What about the generator? Surely there must be a backup power source."

David shook his head, his expression defeated. "The generator's way out in the shed, through that wall of snow ..." He trailed off, his eyes dropping to the floor.

A heavy silence fell over the room. The weight of their situation pressed down on them like a physical force. Emily glanced around at her friends, seeing the fear and uncertainty etched in their faces.

"We need a plan," she signed. "We can't just sit here and wait for the power to come back. We need to be proactive, to take control of the situation."

Scott turned to the group. "Emily's right. We need to take stock of our supplies and resources. Without power, the electronic heaters in the rooms are useless, and we're going to need to find alternative ways to stay warm."

"We've got some firewood left," David said, his forehead sweating, "but it won't last more than a day or two. We might need to start burning furniture and books if the blizzard continues much longer."

Mark's voice shifted at the thought. "It's going to get colder, isn't it? The longer we go without heat ..."

Emily nodded along. "We need to gather everything we can use to stay warm. Blankets, coats—anything that can help insulate us from the cold."

As the group began to discuss their next steps, dividing tasks and assigning roles, Emily felt a rush of anxiety slowly taking over her. She was growing more confident that Alice's killer was still among them. And now, they were in the dark. Who would be next?

As the others began to file out of Emily's room, she frantically dug through her bag, searching for her flashlight. Her movements grew increasingly panicked as she realized it wasn't there. The familiar shape of the torch, which she always kept within easy reach, was conspicuously absent. It was as if someone had intentionally gone through her belongings.

By the time Emily looked up from her fruitless search, the last flickering beam of light was disappearing down the stairs. She was alone, abandoned in the pitch-black hallway, with the chilling knowledge that a killer could be mere feet away.

"Was I next?" The terrifying thought flashed through Emily's mind as she clutched Scott's lighter, her safety in the oppressive darkness.

With trembling hands, Emily flicked the lighter to life. The small flame sputtered, then steadied, casting a feeble glow that barely penetrated the gloom. She took a hesitant step forward, then another, her left hand braced against the wall for support.

The hallway seemed to stretch endlessly before her. Each shadow was a potential hiding place for unseen threats. Emily's breath came in short as she inched her way forward. The lighter's flame danced wildly with each shaky movement, creating grotesque, shifting patterns on the walls.

As she neared the stairs, Emily felt a growing discomfort in her hand. The metal of the lighter, heated by the constant flame, was beginning to burn her thumb and index finger. She gritted her teeth, torn between the pain and her overwhelming fear of the dark. Each second in the blackness felt like an eternity, the pain in her fingers a cruel countdown to when she'd be forced to extinguish her only source of light.

Just as the heat became almost unbearable, Emily saw a faint glow from the foyer below. Relief washed over her, she pressed on, drawn to the promise of light and the presence of others even as uncertainty gnawed at her.

The lighter's flame flickered one last time before Emily was forced to snap it shut; the metal was too hot to hold any longer. For a heart-stopping moment, she was plunged back into total darkness. But now, the subtle illumination from below guided her, a sign of hope in the sea of black that surrounded her.

As Emily descended the stairs, the light grew stronger. She emerged into the foyer. The faint, silvery glow from the snow-covered windows provided just enough light to make out shadowy figures moving about.

The sudden movement caught Emily's eye - David's arm swinging down in a violent arc. Her pulse quickened as she watched him drive the hammer through the window. The glass splintered in a web-like pattern before collapsing inward, fragments scattering across the floor. In the stillness that followed, Emily could feel her heart pounding against her ribs as she stared at David's silhouette, hammer still held in his outstretched hand.

"What the hell, David?" Mark's voice cut through the darkness, a mix of surprise and anger. "Why did it take you so long to do that?"

David's reply was heated, his frustration tangible. "I wasn't exactly thrilled about damaging my vacation home, Mark. But we can't just sit here and wait for help to come."

Emily watched as David cleared away the remaining glass from the window frame. But instead of revealing an escape route, the broken window exposed only a solid wall of snow and ice pressed against the house.

Undeterred, David began to chip away at the compacted snow with the claw of the hammer. The rhythmic sound of metal striking ice filled the air, but it was clear that progress would be excruciatingly slow.

"It's going to take hours to break through this," David grunted, his breath visible in the frigid air now seeping in through the broken window.

Emily shivered, wrapping her arms around herself as she moved past the foyer towards the living room. The sound of splintering wood reached her ears before she entered. In the dim light, she could make out Scott's figure, his muscles straining as he snapped the legs off an antique chair.

"Scott?" Emily signed, catching his attention.

When he looked up, his face was a mix of determination and regret. "We need firewood," he signed back. "The furniture ... It's all we have left."

Emily watched as Claire entered the room, her arms laden with books.

"I found these in the library," Claire announced, her voice tight. "They'll burn, right? We could use them to keep the fire going?"

Their circumstances hit Emily anew. They were burning books and furniture for warmth and smashing windows in a futile attempt to escape—all while a potential killer lurked among them. The darkness that surrounded them mirrored the growing despair in her heart.

As Emily moved farther into the room, she caught sight of Brian huddled near the fireplace, frantically trying to coax a flame from the dying embers. Mark stood nearby where he sorted through a pile of clothes and blankets, preparing for the long, cold night ahead.

The scene before her was one of desperate survival; each person fought against the encroaching cold and the suffocating darkness. But Emily could sense a tidal wave of fear and suspicion.

When the fire finally roared to life and cast a warm glow, the group arranged pillows and blankets on the rug beside the hearth. The makeshift bed was far from comfortable, but it was their best hope for staying warm through the night ahead.

David, having finished pinning a tarp over the broken window to keep out the worst of the chill, made his way back to the group. He found Claire in the kitchen setting a pack of water bottles on the counter. Her movements were sharp and angry, betraying the emotions she was trying to keep in check.

"Need any help?" David asked tentatively, keeping his distance.

Claire's response was immediate and cold. "I'm good," She did not bother to look at him.

David hesitated before taking a deep breath. "Can we talk?"

She whirled around, her eyes flashing with hurt and anger. "About what?" she snapped. "About how you've been planning to leave me? About how you've given up on us?"

David flinched at her words but stood his ground. "Look, I know you're upset, and you have every right to be. But we're in a survival situation here. We need to at least be civil with each other if we're going to make it through this."

Claire laughed bitterly. "Civil! You want me to be civil after you've shattered everything I thought we had?" She paused, her voice dropping to a near whisper. "I love you, David. I'm in love with you. And I can't believe you're just ... quitting. Like our marriage means nothing to you."

David's expression softened, guilt and regret warring with his resolve. "Claire, I'm sorry. I truly am. I never wanted to hurt you. But I meant what I said earlier. Our marriage ... It hasn't been working for a long time."

"You haven't even tried." Claire said, her voice breaking. "You're just giving up."

David sighed heavily. "It's not about giving up, Claire. It's about recognizing when something isn't working and having the courage to move on."

Claire shook her head, tears welling in her eyes. "You don't get to tell me how I feel, David. I want to fight for us. I want to keep trying."

"I understand that," David said gently. "And I'm sorry that I can't give you what you want. But right now, we need to focus on surviving this. We need to work together—all of us—if we're going to make it out of here alive."

For a long moment, Claire said nothing, her eyes fixed on the floor. When she finally looked up, her eyes were filled with a mix of pain and resignation. "Fine," she said with a defeated frustration. "We'll be civil. We'll work together. But don't expect anything more from me. You've made your choice, and now we both have to live with it."

David nodded, understanding the finality in her words. As Claire brushed past him returning to the living room, he couldn't help but feel a pang of regret. He knew he had made the right decision for himself, but seeing Claire's pain made it no less difficult.

Returning to the group huddled around the fire, David was struck by the gravity of their situation. The warmth of the flames did little to dispel the chill of fear and suspicion all around them. As he settled onto the makeshift bed, he looked over to see his friends' faces, illuminated by the flickering firelight.

CHAPTER TEN—Photograph

Brooklyn, New York – 2019

Brian Hansen's heart raced as he sprinted down the grimy steps of the subway station. His camera bag bounced against his hip with each step. The racket of the underground assaulted his senses—the screeching of train wheels, the chatter of impatient commuters, the distant strains of a street musician's saxophone.

"Come on. Come on," he muttered, willing the train to arrive. Each second that ticked by was another nail in the coffin of his dreams. This meeting with Theodore Jameson, editor-in-chief of *Capture* magazine, could make or break his career as a photographer.

The train finally rumbled into the station, and Brian squeezed himself into the packed car, muttering apologies as he jostled fellow passengers. His fingers drummed on his camera bag as the train lurched forward, carrying him toward his destiny.

Emerging from the subway, Brian was immediately swept up in the rushing river of pedestrians on the sidewalk. He weaved through the crowd, muttering "excuse me" and "sorry" as he bumped shoulders and dodged briefcases. The towering skyscrapers loomed above, their glass facades reflecting the morning sun, creating a canyon of light.

Brian's watch taunted him as he finally reached the building. Two minutes late. He took a deep breath, straightened his jacket, and stepped into the sleek lobby of Jameson Publishing House.

The elevator ride to the 30th floor seemed interminable. Brian's reflection in the polished doors stared back at him—a young man with tousled brown hair and anxious green eyes, clutching a portfolio like a lifeline. The doors opened with a soft ding to reveal a reception area that radiated sophistication and success.

"Mr. Jameson will see you now," the receptionist said, her voice clipped and efficient.

Brian stood up, swallowed hard, and approached the imposing oak door. This was it. The moment that could change everything.

Theodore Jameson sat behind a massive desk, his silver hair perfectly coiffed, his steel-blue eyes behind designer glasses. He didn't bother to stand as Brian entered.

"You're late, Hansen," Jameson said, his tone strict.

"I'm so sorry, sir," Brian stammered. "The subway—"

Jameson raised a hand dismissively. "I don't care. You have five minutes, show me what you've got."

With trembling hands, Brian opened his portfolio. He'd spent weeks agonizing over which photos to include, each image carefully selected to showcase his talent and vision. As he laid out the photographs, he explained his artistic approach and the stories behind each shot.

But Jameson barely glanced at the images. He leafed through them quickly, and his frown deepened with each turn of the page. Finally, he looked up at Brian, his eyes cold and unimpressed.

"Hansen," he began, voice dripping with disdain, "what exactly were you hoping to convey with these ... images?"

Brian leaned forward eagerly despite the knot forming in his stomach. "Well, sir, I wanted to capture the *essence* of New York City. The grandeur of the architecture, the—"

"The *essence* of New York?" Jameson interrupted. "Mr. Hansen, these are nothing more than airport postcards. I see a thousand of these everyday and you know what I do? I throw them in the shredder. You've got nothing but soulless pictures and you're wasting time, paper and toner."

Brian felt his heart sink. "I don't understand. Everyone has always loved my—"

Jameson scoffed. "You want to be an artist, then tell me, when you look at these photos, what do you feel? Joy? Fear? Sadness? Because I feel nothing. Nothing. You have a camera, show me that you can use it. Because this isn't art."

"But sir, you have to view it from a technical aspect—" Brian started, only to be cut off again.

"Technical skill means nothing without emotion, without a story." Jameson closed the portfolio with a decisive snap. "Photography isn't just about capturing images, Mr. Hansen. It's about capturing moments, feelings, the very essence of life itself. You're a nice guy, but I'd suggest ditching the camera and working a nice finance gig or something. I don't know what you are, but I'll tell you- you aren't an artist."

Brian sat in stunned silence as Jameson continued, his words cutting deeper with each syllable. "I don't see life in these photos. I see a man hiding behind his camera, afraid to truly connect with his subjects. You are lucky to have my time right now, because clearly nobody else is telling you the truth. Photography ... It's not for you."

The words felt insulting and absolute. Brian mumbled something—a thank you, perhaps, or an apology—and stumbled out of the office, his rejected portfolio clutched to his chest like a shield.

The journey back through the city was a blur. The same crowds that had seemed like obstacles earlier now barely registered. Brian moved through them like a ghost, unseeing and unseen. The subway car, half-empty in the late morning lull, felt cavernous and cold.

Later that day, Brian found himself pushing open the door of a small, dimly lit bar. The neon sign above the door flickered weakly, casting a sickly glow on the wet pavement. Inside, the air was thick with the smell of stale beer and desperation.

Brian slumped into a booth in the corner, his rejected portfolio on the table before him like a tombstone marking his dreams. A small TV mounted in the corner showcased a baseball game. The muted cheers were a crisp contrast to the heavy silence of the near-empty bar.

"What can I get for you?"

Brian looked up to see a petite waitress standing by his table, notepad in hand. Her straight hair was pulled back in a messy ponytail, and her blue eyes sparkled with a warmth that seemed out of place in the gloomy bar.

"Guiness," Brian mumbled. "Tall."

The waitress—*Alice*, according to her name tag—smiled and disappeared. She returned moments later with his drink, setting it down gently in front of him.

"Rough day?" she asked, her voice soft and kind.

Brian nodded, not meeting her eyes. He took a long swig of his beer, relishing the foam as it slid down his throat.

Alice lingered and then seemed to sense his desire for solitude. "Let me know if you need anything else," she said before moving away.

The hours crawled by. Brian nursed his drink and then ordered another. And another. The baseball game ended, replaced by highlights and commentary that blurred into white noise. The bar remained mostly empty, except for a few regulars at the far end.

As Brian contemplated ordering a fourth drink, Alice appeared at his table again. This time, instead of asking for his order, she slid into the seat across from him.

"Mind if I join you?" she asked. "My shift just ended, and you look like you could use some company."

Brian wanted to tell her to leave, that he preferred to wallow in his misery alone. But something in her warm smile made him hesitate.

"Sure," he found himself saying.

Alice beamed. "Great! I'm Alice, by the way. But I guess you already knew that," she added with a chuckle, tapping her nametag.

"Brian," he offered.

"Nice to meet you, Brian," Alice said. "So, want to talk about what's got you drinking alone on a Tuesday night?"

Maybe it was the alcohol, or maybe it was Alice's genuine warmth, but Brian found himself pouring out the whole story. As he spoke, Alice listened attentively, her expression shifting between sympathy and indignation on his behalf.

"That Jameson guy sounds like a real jerk," Alice said when he finished. "I mean, who is he to crush someone's dreams like that?"

Brian shrugged. "Maybe he's right. Maybe I'm just fooling myself thinking I could actually make it as a photographer."

Alice's eyes narrowed. "Now that's just the beer talking. Come on, let me see these photos he was so quick to dismiss."

Hesitantly, Brian slid the portfolio towards her. Alice opened it, her smile growing as she took in each image. As she turned the pages, her usual chatter fell away, replaced by a reverent silence.

"Brian," she finally said, looking up at him with awe, "these are ... incredible. The way you've captured the light here, and the perspective in this one ... I've lived in New York for a few years now, and you've captured it exactly right."

Brian felt a warmth spreading through his chest that had nothing to do with the alcohol. "You don't mean that."

Alice placed her hand on his emphatically. "Absolutely. This Jameson guy? He doesn't know what he's talking about. You have a real talent, Brian. Don't let anyone tell you otherwise."

For the first time that day, Brian felt a glimmer of hope. They talked for hours, the conversation flowing easily from photography to their backgrounds and dreams.

"So, where are you from?" Brian asked, finding himself genuinely curious about this vibrant woman who had breathed life back into his deflated spirit.

Alice's smile turned a bit wistful. "I grew up in a small town called Glenwood, up in Northern Utah. It's beautiful there—all rugged hills and the sweetest people. I was raised by my grandparents after my parents passed."

"I'm sorry to hear that," Brian said softly.

Alice shrugged. "It's okay. My grandparents were wonderful. They're the ones who encouraged me to come to New York, to chase my dreams of performing on Broadway. What about you? Where does Brian Hansen come from?"

"Chicago," Brian replied. "Grew up there with my parents. They ... Well, let's just say they had very specific ideas about what constitutes a 'proper' career. But I fell in love with photography in high school, and I couldn't imagine doing anything else. So I applied to art school behind their backs."

Alice's eyes fluttered. "Wow, that must have taken some guts. How'd they take it?"

"Not well, at first. But they came around eventually. I think they're still hoping I'll 'grow out of it' and go to law school or something." Brian chuckled.

As the first light of dawn began to creep through the windows, Brian found himself asking, "Would you like to have dinner with me tomorrow night?"

Alice's smile was radiant. "I'd love to."

The following evening, Brian found himself sitting across from Alice at a small Italian restaurant, the candlelight casting a warm glow on her face. As they shared a meal of pasta and wine, their conversation picked up right where it had left off.

"So, tell me more about Glenwood," Brian said, twirling spaghetti around his fork. "I imagine it was a bit nicer than the cold city of Chicago?"

Alice's eyes lit up. "Oh, it was magical. The kind of place where everyone knows everyone else. We had this little library right on the edge of town, and I used to spend hours there, reading everything I could get my hands on. And the lake! Beautiful lake! We'd have bonfires in the summer, telling ghost stories and roasting marshmallows."

Brian smiled, captivated by the picture she painted. "Sounds idyllic. So different from life here in the big apple."

"You have no idea." Alice laughed. "What was it like for you, growing up in the city?"

Brian shrugged. "It had its moments. The Art Institute was my sanctuary—I'd spend whole weekends there, just soaking it all in. But it could be lonely too, you know? Honestly it's not too different from New York. In a city this big, it's easy to feel invisible."

Alice grabbed his hand softly, a new habit she picked up. "Well, I see you, Brian Hansen. And I think you're pretty special."

As they continued to talk, sharing stories and dreams, Brian felt something shift inside him. The sting of Jameson's rejection began to fade, replaced by a growing sense of possibility. With Alice's unwavering belief in him and his own rekindled passion, he began to see a future where his photography could flourish.

As the evening drew to a close, Brian walked Alice to her apartment. Standing on the stoop and bathed in the warm glow of the streetlight, he felt an overwhelming urge to capture this moment.

"Do you mind if I ...?" he asked, gesturing to his ever-present camera.

Alice smiled and nodded. Brian raised the camera to his eye, framing Alice against the backdrop of the city he loved. As he pressed the shutter, he knew that this image—and this night—would stay with him forever.

The crackling fire cast shifting shadows across the living room of the Belmont Lodge. Emily sat reading more and more of Lily's diary when she stopped for a moment to look at Brian, who lay on the floor near the hearth, his stare fixed on the ceiling. The flickering flames highlighted the hollowness in his cheeks, the dark circles under his eyes. Emily felt a harsh pang of sympathy for him, for she knew the depth of his loss.

Shaking off these thoughts, Emily returned her attention to Lily's diary. The leather-bound book felt heavy in her hands, weighted with secrets from the past. She turned the page, and her lips shook as she read the next entry.

February 15, 1893

I have come to understand a great truth about this lodge and the people who dwell within its walls. There are two kinds of souls in this world: the Lights and the Shadows.

The Lights are those whose hearts shine with goodness. They exist to serve others, to protect and nurture. Their presence brings warmth and comfort, like the gentle glow of a candle in the darkness. They are the ones who make this world a better place, often at great cost to themselves.

Then there are the Shadows. These are the souls consumed by darkness, existing only to further their desires. They care not for whom they hurt or what they destroy in their pursuit of power and success. Their hearts are cold, their smiles false, and their words poison disguised as honey.

This lodge, with its grand facade and hidden passages, seems to attract both. But beware, for in this place, the line between light and shadow blurs. Even those who believe themselves to be Lights may find darkness growing within their hearts ...

Emily sat back, her mind reeling from Lily's words. She glanced around the room at her friends, seeing them in a new way. If there was something supernatural at hand, the lodge was teasing each of them. Of course, she wanted to believe they were each good, light, but for someone to perform such evil and put on a full performance for days, they must be harnessing some kind of explicit evil, a shadow. Pulling out a pen, she began to make notes in the margin of the diary.

"Alice—L" Emily didn't hesitate. Alice had been kind, genuine, and caring. Even in death, her light seemed to linger.

"Scott—L" Another easy choice. Scott's unwavering support and courage to protect everyone solidified his status.

"Claire—?" Emily paused. The Claire she thought she knew would undoubtedly be a Light, but lately ... Her erratic behavior and the tension with David gave Emily pause.

"David—?" She wanted to believe in his inherent goodness, but recent revelations cast doubt. His marital problems, his suspicious interaction with Alice, and the fact that he'd been downstairs that night all weighed heavily against him.

"Brian—L" Emily felt a twinge of sadness as she wrote this. Brian's devastation at losing Alice felt genuine, and what she knew of his past showed a man who had persevered through hardship to pursue his dreams.

"Mark—?" Emily hesitated. Mark's anger issues and past behavior made him hard to categorize. His recent aggression was concerning, but was it born of grief or something darker?

"Meredith—?" The evidence pointed to Meredith being a Shadow, but something about that conclusion felt wrong to Emily. Meredith had always seemed kind, perhaps a bit reserved. Was she actually capable of murder?

As Emily reviewed her notes, she realized how little she truly knew about her friends' current lives. They had all changed since high school and grown in ways she couldn't have anticipated. She had no clue who they really were, beneath the surface.

She thought about Alice's apparent desire to leave Brian. About David's failing marriage and his regrettable interaction with Alice. About Mark's underlying anger and Claire's erratic behavior. About Meredith's supposed confession and suicide.

Every piece of information seemed to contradict the next. Emily felt like she was trying to complete a puzzle with half the pieces missing and the other half from different sets entirely.

She looked around the room again and studied each face carefully. The firelight cast shadows that seemed to scatter across their faces, alternately highlighting and obscuring. It was as if the lodge itself was playing with her perceptions, blurring the lines between light and shadow just as Lily had written.

The pale light of dawn crept through the frost-covered windows of the Belmont Lodge, casting long shadows across the silent halls. Emily found Claire in the kitchen, rummaging through cabinets with a frustrated sigh.

"Need some help?" Emily signed as she approached.

Claire jumped slightly and then offered a weak smile. "Yeah, thanks. I'm trying to figure out how to make breakfast without power." Just then, Claire remembered the propane grill stored in the basement. "There's a grill downstairs. We could use that."

Emily let out a friendly smile. "Good thinking. Let's go get it."

As they descended the basement stairs, Emily felt a chill that had nothing to do with the temperature. The image of Meredith's body, lifeless and accusing, flashed through her mind.

Claire seemed to sense Emily's discomfort. "Let's make this quick," she muttered.

They found the grill and hurried back upstairs, but the oppressive atmosphere of the basement clung to them like a shroud. While they set up the grill in the kitchen, Emily broached the subject that had been weighing on her.

"Claire," she signed, her movements hesitant, "can I ask you something about Alice?"

Claire tensed visibly but shrugged. "Sure. What about her?"

Emily took a deep breath. "Were you and Alice ... okay? I mean, before everything happened over dinner that night. Did you notice anything different about her?"

Claire's hands stilled over the grill. "Honestly Emily, what are you getting at?"

"I just ... I can't help feeling like we're missing something. Like there's more to what happened than we know."

Claire's expression hardened, and her lips began to move with exaggerated precision—the kind of over-pronunciation Emily had learned to recognize since childhood. It wasn't the careful enunciation of someone trying to be understood; it was the patronizing slowness people used when they thought being deaf meant being stupid.

"Stop making this into something it isn't," Claire shouted. "We know what happened. Meredith killed Alice and then took her own life out of guilt. It's horrible, but it's not some grand mystery."

She leaned forward, each word now almost comically overemphasized. "You need to accept this, Emily. We can't properly grieve Alice if we're busy playing detective. I know you think you're being clever, but sometimes things are exactly what they seem."

Emily pressed on, undeterred. "But what about Meredith's behavior before? Did you notice anything strange? And Alice. Was she acting differently towards anyone?"

Claire slammed the grill lid shut. The sound echoed in the crisp morning air. "Enough, Emily. You're seeing mysteries where there aren't any. Nothing sinister is going on anymore. Meredith killed Alice, and the sooner you can accept that, the sooner you can move on. It's hard, but we all need to face the facts."

Emily felt a flicker of frustration. "Claire, if we just look a little deeper—"

"I said enough!" Claire snapped. "I can't do this with you right now. I'm going to my room. You can make your own breakfast if you want."

With that, Claire stormed off, leaving Emily alone in the kitchen. Emily watched her go, suspicion swirling in her gut. She hadn't meant to upset Claire, but her friend's reaction seemed disproportionate to the questions.

As Emily turned back to the grill, her mind raced. Claire's defensiveness, her insistence on accepting the simplest explanation, her refusal to even consider other possibilities—it all pointed to someone with something to *hide*.

With a heavy heart, Emily made a choice to update her list. Next to Claire's name, she erased the question mark and wrote "S." The act brought her no joy, only a deepening sense of unease.

Emily realized that solving this wasn't just about categorizing people as good or evil. It was about understanding the complexities of human nature, the capacity for both *good* and *darkness* that existed within each of them. As difficult as it was to imagine, Claire could be capable of horrendous evil.

As she prepared her breakfast alone, Emily couldn't shake the feeling that she was running out of time. The truth was out there, hidden in the shadows, and she had to uncover it before it was too late.

Emily saw Mark sitting alone by the window. Staring at the crushing weight of snow pressed against the house. She approached cautiously, still unsure of where he stood in her mental categorization.

"Hey," she signed. "Can we talk?"

Mark nodded, but his expression was guarded. "What's on your mind?"

Emily took a deep breath. "I wanted to ask you about Claire and Alice. Did you notice anything ... off between them before everything happened?"

Mark's shoulders raised. "Off? Not really. I mean, Claire and Alice were always close, but they had their own lives, you know?"

"And what about you and Alice? Were you close?"

Mark shrugged, his response surprisingly nonchalant. "Not particularly. We were friendly, sure, but we never really connected on a deeper level. She was more Claire's friend than mine."

Emily let out a friendly smirk. It seemed anticlimactic, almost too simple. But as she studied Mark's face, she saw no signs of deception, no hint of hidden depths or secret knowledge.

"Thanks, Mark," she signed. "I appreciate your honesty."

Mark let out a soft chuckle. "Isn't it a little redundant to ask these questions now? I mean, it's over."

Emily didn't want to expose her stance. She was strongly convinced Meredith and Alice's killer was lurking in the lodge. "You're right. Sorry." She let out a disingenuous smile. "Curious, is all."

Mark turned back to the window, and Emily took out her notepad and revised her list. Next to Mark's name, she erased the question mark and added an "L." His lack of connection to Alice and his straightforward answers suggested he likely had nothing to do with her death or Meredith's.

Just as Emily was about to walk away, she saw Scott's panicked gestures. "Guys! Something's wrong with Brian!"

Emily and Mark rushed to where Brian lay near the fireplace. He was trembling and covered in cold sweat, his skin pale and clammy. Scott was kneeling beside him.

"His speech was slurring a bit, and then he just collapsed," Scott signed tensely. Without hesitation, he checked Brian's pulse, finding it rapid but weak. Brian's eyes were unfocused, and his movements were jerky and uncoordinated.

As the seconds ticked by, Emily's mind raced. Brian had barely eaten since finding Alice's body, surviving only on coffee and refusing all food. The grief had consumed him completely.

"It's got to be his blood sugar," Scott signed. "I don't think he's eaten in days." With a grunt of effort, Scott lifted Brian's limp form and began carrying him up the stairs.

Claire rushed to the kitchen, returning with orange juice and honey. Her earlier anger was forgotten in the face of this medical emergency. She hurried upstairs with the supplies.

Emily followed Scott, her heart pounding. As Scott laid Brian on a bed, she could see him drifting in and out of consciousness, his confusion evident.

"Is he going to be alright?" Emily signed, her hands shaking.

Scott began administering small amounts of juice. "Severe hypoglycemia," he signed with one hand. "We need to get his blood sugar up slowly. If he doesn't improve soon, this could become dangerous."

"How long has it been since anyone's seen him eat?" David asked, his voice tight.

"He's barely touched anything since..." Emily's signs trailed off, not needing to finish the sentence. They all knew since when. A heavy silence fell over the room as the implications sank in. Grief could destroy a person in more ways than one.

"We need to get out of here," Mark said, voicing what they were all thinking.

David nodded, his jaw set with calculation. "I'm going to keep working on breaking through the ice. This is ridiculous. We can't wait for help anymore. Clearly nobody is coming for us. We need to make our own way out of here."

As David headed for the foyer, pick in hand, Emily couldn't help but feel a sense of dread. They were racing against time on multiple fronts now—the cold, the dwindling supplies, Brian's deteriorating condition, and the lingering presence of a potential killer in their midst.

She looked around at her friends, each face etched with worry and exhaustion. The lines between Lights and Shadows seemed to blur even further in the face of this new crisis. As David's pick struck ice, Emily realized that their survival might depend on working together, regardless of each other's secrets.

Emily jogged up the stairs with a flashlight in hand to check on Brian. "Hey, you doing okay?"

Brian's eyes remained disoriented for a moment, "Oh, hey Emily. It's nice of you to check up on me. I'm doing okay, Scott said it was probably my blood sugar." The room was illuminated by a dozen candles.

"Yeah, you have to eat food, Brian."

He let out a single laugh, "I guess so, huh."

"Well, I'm just glad you're conscious again. David's working on getting us out of here."

"How? I thought the ice-"

"You should see him. He's chiseling out chunks of ice in the foyer. I think he's angry and it's helping."

Brian smiled, "You're a good friend. I'm doing okay up here, thanks for thinking of me."

"Of course. We'll be right downstairs, if you need anything at all. But you should probably stay in bed."

"I'm not going anywhere." Brian said, before coughing.

Emily swiftly moved back down the stairs, her flashlight aiming at every dark corner. At the foot of the stairs, the floor was becoming wet. Chunks of ice, some as big as a basketball scattered everywhere. David wasn't even in the lodge anymore, his feet barely visible as he carved the way out of the broken window. Their escape was getting closer.

Emily's thoughts lingered on Brian's condition. Then, she noticed his camera lying on the floor where he had collapsed. Gently, she picked it up, remembering how he'd been documenting their entire trip. She paused for a moment before having a seat on the couch. She didn't mean to snoop around his personal belongings, but he had been taking pictures this whole trip and she just wanted to see Alice's perfect smile. Surprisingly the battery was still half-full. As she clicked through the photos, each image told a story of their time here – before everything went wrong. The lodge's intricate details captured in stunning clarity, preserved memories of happiness that now felt like they belonged to someone else.

Her breath caught as she found recent photos of Alice in the lodge. Her smooth skin glowed in the light, her innocent smile radiating warmth. Brian had captured these moments perfectly, preserving the spirit of Alice's presence—her joy, her light, her life. Each image was a painful reminder of all they had lost.

Just as Emily was clicking through photos, David's excited shout echoed through the lodge. "Guys! I think there's enough of a gap—We can get out!"

CHAPTER ELEVEN—Escape

David captured the attention of everyone in the living room

with his announcement.

The news electrified the group. Scott and Mark rushed to join David at the makeshift exit he had created. The window frame was jagged with shards of glass still clinging to the edges. Beyond the wall of packed snow that David had spent hours aggressively breaking apart, creating a tunnel just wide enough to crawl through.

"It's tight, but I think we can make it," David said, his breath clouding in the frigid air as he crawled back into the lodge.

Scott nodded. "I'll go first. Mark, you follow, and David, you bring up the rear."

Before they left, Claire pulled David aside for a private moment. "Be careful. Remember there's a gas station up the road?"

"Yeah, they should have a working phone or at least a radio we can use," David replied.

Emily wrapped Scott in a tight hug. "Go save the day."

Scott drew her aside, speaking quietly, "My gun is in your bag, just in case."

Emily's lips quirked into a small smile. "Don't you mean *weapon*? I thought guns were toys?" she teased, trying to lighten the moment.

Scott's expression remained serious. "I love you. I'll be right back."

Without waiting for another response, Scott began to squeeze through the opening. The snow pressed in on all sides, cold and unyielding. For a moment, claustrophobia threatened to overwhelm him, but he pushed through, inch by painstaking inch.

"You know," Mark's voice drifted from behind, strained with effort, "I should've stayed back."

David's chuckle turned into a grunt as he navigated a particularly tight spot. "Please don't stop, Mark, your ass is much closer to my face than I'd like."

"All right, keep moving," Scott called back, his voice muffled by the snow. "Impressive little tunnel you made here, David."

David shouted, "Thanks, anything to get out of that damn place."

Their conversation, punctuated by grunts of effort and the scrape of clothing against snow, helped to keep the panic at bay.

Finally, after what felt like hours but was likely only minutes, Scott felt the tunnel widening. With a final push, he burst through the last of the snow wall, tumbling onto the surface. He quickly scrambled to his feet, turning to help Mark emerge.

"Come on, man," Scott said. He gripped Mark's arms and pulled. "Almost there."

With a groan, Mark popped free, rolled onto his back, and breathed heavily. David followed shortly after, his face red with exertion.

When they stood and brushed snow from their clothes, the three men fell silent, awestruck by the scene before them. The world was a blank canvas of white, the boundary between snow-covered ground and overcast sky nearly indiscernible. It was as if they had emerged into a different dimension, a realm of pure, blinding whiteness.

"My God," David whispered, "I never thought I'd be so happy to see the open sky."

Scott nodded and squinted against the glare. "It's beautiful—in a terrifying sort of way. I can't even tell where the ground ends and the sky begins."

Mark turned in a slow circle. "How are we supposed to find our way in this?"

The question was valid. Around them stretched nothing but an endless downhill slope of white. The lodge had vanished completely beneath the snow, with only the black chimney pipe sticking up like a lone protector. At least that would serve as their beacon—all they knew was they had to head downhill, and they could find their way back by following that solitary black pipe piercing the white landscape.

Scott pulled his phone from his pocket only to find a black, lifeless screen. The battery had long since died during their time spent without power.

"We need to get down to the main road," Scott said, pointing towards where he thought the main highway should be. "It's our best chance of finding help."

Carefully, the three men began to make their way down the slope. The snow was deep and treacherous, each step a gamble between finding solid footing and sinking knee-deep into a drift.

They had made it about halfway down when disaster struck. Mark, a few paces ahead, lost his footing on a patch of ice hidden beneath the snow. With a startled cry, he pitched forward. His body picked up speed as he slid down the steep incline.

"Mark!" Scott shouted, instinctively lunging forward to help. But the sudden movement threw off his precarious balance, and he too slid uncontrollably down the mountain.

David, witnessing his friends' predicament, tried to maintain his footing, but the combination of deep snow and hidden ice proved too much. Within seconds, all three men were careening down the slope. Their world became a dizzying blur of white punctuated by the occasional painful collision with buried rocks or branches.

After what seemed like an eternity of tumbling and sliding, they mercifully came to rest on a level patch of ground. Groaning, they slowly picked themselves up, checking for injuries.

"Everyone okay?" Scott asked, wincing as he rotated his shoulder.

Mark pushed himself up and combed the snow out of his hair. "Yeah, I think so. Nothing broken, at least."

David stood up, grimacing. "I'm going to have some impressive bruises, but I'll live. That was ... not how I planned to get down the mountain."

Despite the pain and the cold, a bubble of laughter rose in Scott's chest. Soon, all three men were chuckling, the absurdity of their situation momentarily overwhelming the danger and fear they had been living with for days.

As their laughter subsided, they took stock of their surroundings. The unending emptiness stretched in all directions, except for the vague, dark shapes of distant trees.

"We need to find the road," David said, and his expression grew serious once more. "But in this ... How do we know which way to go?"

Scott squinted, trying to make out any landmarks in the featureless landscape. Just as he was about to suggest picking a direction at random, a gust of wind parted the swirling snow, revealing a faint shape in the distance.

"Look!" he exclaimed, pointing. "Is that ... a sign?"

The three men peered through the snowy haze. Slowly, the shape resolved itself into a battered road sign, its edges caked with ice.

Mark stepped closer and brushed away the snow that obscured the writing. "It's ... It's pointing to a gas station! Two miles that way."

David's eyes lit up with hope. "Oh yeah, little diesel place down the road! We aren't that far, and there's gotta be a phone there or something."

Scott nodded, a surge of energy coursing through him despite his exhaustion. "It's our best shot. Come on, let's go."

With renewed motivation, the three men set off in the direction indicated by the sign. The promise of civilization, of help, of an end to their ordeal, drove them through the endless nothingness.

As they trudged through the deep snow, the wind occasionally parting to reveal glimpses of their destination, Scott couldn't shake the feeling that their ordeal was far from over. The gas station might offer a lifeline to the outside world, long awaited help for their situation back at the lodge.

The thin trail of smoke rising from a distant chimney served as their beacon, guiding them through the blank canvas of the winter landscape.

Back at the lodge, an uneasy silence had settled over the living room. Emily sat on the couch where she absently flipped through the pictures on Brian's camera. Claire stared out the broken window at the narrow tunnel. The crackling of the fire was the only sound breaking the stillness.

Finally, Claire spoke softly, "I wonder how far the guys have gotten."

Emily looked up from the photos to sign. "Hopefully they've made it to some kind of shelter by now. This weather is brutal."

Claire agreed softly and turned away from the window. "Yeah, I just hope they're safe."

A comfortable silence fell between them for a moment. Then, almost as if thinking aloud, Emily signed, "You know, I've been trying to piece together everything that happened that night. It's all such a blur."

Claire's posture stiffened slightly, but her voice remained casual. "What do you mean?"

Emily's eyes zeroed in concentration. "Just trying to remember the sequence of events. When exactly did you say you went to bed that night?"

"Last night?" Claire asked, a hint of confusion in her voice.

Emily shook her head. "No, um ... the night everything happened with Alice."

Claire's expression darkened, and her tone changed. "Why are you asking about this again?"

"I'm just trying to understand—" Emily began to sign, but Claire cut her off.

"No, you're not just trying to understand. You're obsessing," Claire snapped. "Why can't you let this go? We've been over it a hundred times."

Emily's hands moved faster, her signs becoming more emphatic. "Because it doesn't add up. There are too many inconsistencies, too many unanswered questions."

Claire stood up abruptly, and her voice rose. "The only question here is why you can't move on. Alice is dead, and Meredith's suicide is a clear confession. It's horrible, but it's over. You need to accept that. I'm tired of talking in circles with you."

Emily felt a surge of frustration. She stood as well. Her signs became more decisive. "How can you be so sure? Why are you so resistant to even considering other possibilities?"

"Because your 'possibilities' are nothing but paranoid delusions!" Claire shouted. Her face flushed with anger. "You're so desperate to play detective that you're seeing everyone as some kind of conspiring villain, but you're ignoring straight-up facts."

Emily pressed on, undeterred. "If you don't have anything to hide, why not help me investigate? Why insist on accepting this convenient *murder-suicide* explanation?"

Claire's eyes narrowed dangerously. "You've lost your mind. Do you hear yourself? You sound crazy."

"I'm not crazy," Emily signed, her movements becoming more agitated. "I'm trying to find the truth. For Alice. Why does that scare you so much?"

Something in Claire snapped. With a cry of rage, she lunged forward and shoved Emily hard. Caught off guard by the sudden aggression, Emily stumbled backward. Her knee painfully smacked against the edge of the coffee table before she hit the ground.

"You need help," Claire spat. Her voice trembled with anger and what sounded like fear. "Stay the hell away from me. And stay out of things you don't understand."

Emily looked up at Claire from the floor, shock and hurt evident in her expression. She had known Claire for years and had considered her one of her closest friends. This violent outburst was so out of character that it only served to deepen Emily's suspicions.

"Claire," Emily said, her signs slow as she pushed herself up. "What aren't you telling me? What are you so afraid of?"

For a moment, something flickered in Claire's eyes—a flash of vulnerability, possibly fear. But it was quickly replaced by cold, hard anger. "I'm not afraid of anything. I'm tired of your paranoid delusions. Alice is *dead*. End of story. If you can't accept that, if you insist on dragging us all through this nightmare over and over again, then you're not the friend I thought you were."

With that, Claire turned on her heel and stormed upstairs. Emily was left alone in the living room, her knee throbbing and her mind reeling from the confrontation. Perhaps their conversations were not productive anymore. She had to agree, it felt like they were talking in circles. Maybe Claire was guilty, or maybe she was just annoyed from all the questioning. Scott was finished with the investigation, but Emily just felt like she was a step away from figuring this out. It was right in front of her, she just had to keep digging.

Scott, Mark, and David trudged through the deep snow. Their breaths came in as heavy huffs. The storm had abated somewhat, but the wind still bit at their exposed skin, and the snow reached past their knees. They followed the faint smoke rising in the distance, their last option in the endless sea of snow.

"Here we go," Mark shouted and pointed ahead. Through the swirling snow, they could make out the dim outline of a building.

As they drew closer, they saw it was a small gas station. Its neon "OPEN" sign flickered weakly. The smoke they had been following curled up from a rusty chimney pipe.

The three men stumbled through the door, bringing a gust of cold air and snow with them. The warmth of the interior hit them like a physical force, and their cold-numb skin tingled painfully.

An old man stood behind the counter with a wandering eye. He regarded them with a mixture of surprise and suspicion. His gnarled hands hesitated while restocking a shelf of beef jerky.

"What in tarnation?" the old man muttered. His good eye narrowed at their snow-covered forms. "You boys look like you've been through hell and back."

Scott, shaking snow from his coat, stepped forward. "Sir, we need to use your phone. It's an emergency."

The old man focused on Scott. "Phone's for paying customers only," he drawled, a note of curiosity in his voice.

The shopkeeper shuffled closer, his wandering eye fixed unnervingly on them while the other drifted without direction. "Ain't natural," he muttered, more to himself than them. "Walking around out there..."

Scott exchanged a wary glance with Mark. The old man continued, "I've been here forty years." He began restacking cans that were already perfectly aligned."

David's face had gone pale. "Sir, we really just need to use the phone."

The old man's good eye fixed on David. "You're one of them Belmont's, ain't you? Can see it in your face. You've got the look..." He left the sentence hanging, heavy with judgment.

David interjected, "Just- we'll take three coffees, please. As hot as you can make them."

The shopkeeper nodded slowly but still eyed them warily. "All right then. You fellas want to tell me what you're doing out in this godforsaken weather?"

As the old man shuffled off to prepare their drinks, Scott grabbed the phone on the counter and began to dial 911. Mark and David moved closer, forming a protective circle around Scott as he waited for the call to connect.

"911, what's your emergency?" came the calm voice on the other end.

Scott's words tumbled out in a rush. "We need help at 667 Willow road. There are two dead bodies, and we've been trapped by the snow for five days. Please send someone immediately."

The operator's voice sharpened. "Sir, can you please repeat that? Did you say dead bodies?"

"Yes," Scott confirmed, clearing his throat. "Two dead bodies, our friends are still there. It's a long story, but we need police and medical assistance right away. We've been cut off from the outside world for almost a week."

As Scott continued to relay information to the 9-1-1 operator, the old shopkeeper returned with their coffees. His wrinkled hands shook as he set them down.

"What's all this about dead bodies?" he asked. "Are you boys in some kind of trouble?"

Mark stepped in. "It's been a hectic few days. We'd rather not talk about it if you don't mind."

David sipped his coffee and then attempted to change the subject. "This is good coffee. You must get a lot of travelers stopping by."

The shopkeeper snorted. "Ain't had a customer in days on account of the blizzard. You boys are the first living souls I've seen all week."

His choice of words sent a chill down Scott's spine that had nothing to do with their recent trek through the snow.

With the assurance that help was on the way, Scott picked up his coffee and began to make his way toward the door. "We need to get back to the lodge," he said to Mark and David. "The others need to know help is coming."

The three men gulped down their coffee, the hot liquid a welcome respite from the cold. As they prepared to head back out, the old shopkeeper called out to them, "Now you boys be careful out there." His wandering eye seemed to follow them independently of his good one. "Easy to get lost in all the-"

His cryptic warning was cut off as Scott, Mark, and David pushed their way back out into the swirling snow.

Emily sat alone in the living room. Her confrontation with Claire replayed in her mind. The violence of Claire's reaction had shaken her to her core, pushing Claire to the top of her list of suspects. With trembling hands, she picked up Brian's camera, hoping to find some evidence.

Emily's breath caught in her throat while she clicked through the photos. Brian's skill as a photographer was evident in every shot. Alice's radiant smile beamed from the screen, her beauty captured in various settings around the lodge. As tears rolled down Emily's cheek.

Image after image flickered before her eyes. The majestic exterior of the lodge. The intricate details of the paintings. And then, in the background of one photo, Emily spotted something that made her pause. Claire, her expression tight and judgmental, watched as Brian photographed Alice. The camera had caught a moment of naked emotion on Claire's face—jealousy, anger, and possibly something darker.

Emily's mind raced as she pieced together a motive. She remembered the fight Claire and Alice had had the night of the murder and Claire's suspicions about David and Alice having an affair. While Emily knew those suspicions were unfounded, the perceived betrayal could have pushed Claire over the edge.

I've known Claire since grade school, Emily thought to herself. Her hands clenched around the camera. *But under the right circumstances ... Who knows what any of us are capable of?*

She thought of Mark, Claire's twin brother, and their family's history of violence. The pieces were falling into place, painting an ugly picture with Claire at its center. There had been signs all along, her defensive response to Emily's doubts, her controlling demeanor, how she'd been the first to find Alice's body. Even the way she treated Meredith more like a slave than staff now seemed significant. This whole grieving friend act—was it just that, an act? Emily remembered how Claire had thrown up after discovering Meredith's body, but had anyone actually watched her? She could have easily forced herself to vomit, making sure everyone saw her distress.

Emily's finger hesitated over the button as she scrolled through more photos. There was Alice, smiling with her oldest friends, completely unaware of the horror that would unfold. Emily made a mental note to ask Brian for these files once they escaped—these might be their last happy memories together. Then something strange caught her eye. A dark photo, clearly taken at night. Emily squinted at it, then felt her blood run cold. It was her—asleep in her bed.

She clicked forward, her hands beginning to shake. More photos of herself sleeping. Then Scott's peaceful form illuminated by moonlight, Claire curled up in her sheets, Mark sprawled across his mattress. Photo after photo, all of them sleeping, vulnerable, unaware. Each click of the button revealed another violation of trust.

That figure in her doorway that night—it hadn't been a dream. It was Brian, camera in hand. He was upstairs right now, being cared for by Claire. But why? What purpose could these photos serve? The intimacy of the invasion made her skin crawl. Brian, who they'd been so worried about, who they'd been protecting—had been stalking them in such most vulnerable moments.

With growing dread, she clicked forward again, and there it was, Alice's lifeless body, exactly as they had found her.

Her hands shook as she continued scrolling through the photos. Each image revealed Brian's descent into obsession. Early shots showed Alice laughing, natural and carefree. But as the timestamps progressed, the photos became more predatory—Alice caught unaware, her face in profile, shadows emphasizing her vulnerability. The shift was subtle but unmistakable, like watching a hunter stalk his prey.

What disturbed Emily most was the artistry of it all. Even in the most invasive shots, Brian's technical skill was evident. The composition, the lighting, the way he captured moments of unconscious vulnerability—it was beautiful in its violation. Emily felt bile rise in her throat as she realized that to Brian, their privacy, their trust, their lives were nothing but materials for his twisted vision.

As she stared at the horrific image, something caught her eye that she hadn't noticed before. The timestamp on the photo: 1:14 a.m. Emily's pulse quickened as she zoomed in.

Quickly, she clicked back through the photos to find the last one taken of Alice alive at the dinner table. The timestamp read 10:43 p.m. Emily recalled that morning when Claire's scream had woken them all around 5 AM. The fireplace had been freshly stoked then, embers still glowing hot from new logs. But in this photo from 1:14 AM, she could see those same logs just being placed in the grate.

Emily's thoughts raced. Why would there be a photo of Alice's body taken hours before they discovered her? The group had been asleep; no one should have known about Alice's death until morning.

A realization flashed in her mind. The only person who could have taken that photo was the person always behind the camera: *Brian*.

The camera slipped in her trembling hands. Brian had killed Alice and framed Meredith. The timestamps on the photos, the carefully staged scene, his convenient documentation of everything—it all pointed to him. His supposed grief, his lack of appetite—it wasn't trauma at all. It was guilt.

He had strangled Alice, then played his part perfectly to slip below their radar. Emily's heart began to race as another realization struck. That she and Claire were alone in the lodge with him right now. As tempting as it was to crawl through the escape route David had carved, she couldn't leave Claire up there, unknowingly under the same roof as a killer.

CHAPTER TWELVE—Killer

Everything had become a frozen scope of white, breaking by the dark silhouettes of three men battling against the relentless storm. Scott, Mark, and David pushed forward. Each step was a struggle against the knee-deep snow and raging storm. The warmth of the gas station was now just a memory. The bitter cold seeped through their clothes and into their bones.

Scott took the lead, his police training kicking in. He forged a path through the deepest drifts. Every few minutes, he turned to check on the others, all barely visible through the swirling snow.

Mark followed closely. His skinny build did not serve him well in the tight burying snow. David brought up the rear, his breath coming in freezing gasps.

"How much farther?" Mark shouted, his words nearly lost in the wind's howl.

Scott paused and squinted against the stinging snow as he tried to get his bearings. The landscape was endless and really had no discernible landmarks. "Can't be more than a mile now," he called back. He hoped he sounded more confident than he felt. "We just need to keep moving."

They pressed on. The silence between them was filled by the crunch of snow beneath their feet and the occasional grunt of exertion.

David stumbled and fell to one knee. Mark moved to help him up. Brushing snow away from his coat, he asked, "You okay?"

David coughed, his face pale with exhaustion. "Just ... Just need a moment," he gasped.

Scott backtracked to join them. "We can't stop for long." He eyed the sky warily. "The storm's getting worse. If we don't make it back soon, we might not make it back at all."

As if to emphasize his point, a gust of wind whipped around them, momentarily obscuring their vision. When it cleared, David straightened up, a new determination in his eyes. "You're right." He took a deep breath. "Let's go."

They resumed their trek, each step a battle against nature's fury. The cold seemed to seep into their very souls. Time lost all meaning.

Scott's voice broke through the monotony of their march. "Do you think the others are alright?"

Mark turned. "I'm sure they're fine. Probably worried sick about us, though."

David chimed in, "At least they're safe and warm inside. And with Meredith ... gone ... they don't have to worry about anything too crazy."

The men fell silent again, each contemplating the bizarre turn of events that had led them to this point. The tragedy of Alice's death, the shock of Meredith's confession and suicide—it all seemed surreal now as they battled against the elements.

David called out, his voice tight with excitement. "Hey guys, isn't that the chimney pipe?"

Through a brief parting in the swirling snow, they caught a glimpse of the metallic chimney flue looming against the white backdrop. The Belmont Lodge was finally within sight.

A surge of energy coursed through the men. They quickened their pace. As they drew closer, details began to emerge from the snowy haze—the outline of the roof and the dim glow of windows.

"We made it," Scott breathed.

Mark grinned despite his tiredness. "I can't wait to tell them we got through to 911. We're finally getting out of here."

David nodded, and a weak smile crossed his face.

As they approached the lodge, their thoughts were primarily on the warmth awaiting them inside and the good news they were bringing. However, when they neared the spot where they had originally emerged, a new problem presented itself. The tunnel they had painstakingly crawled through was nowhere to be seen. The relentless storm had filled it in, leaving only a smooth blanket of white in its wake.

"No, no, no," David muttered. "Where's the opening?"

Scott stepped forward. "It has to be here somewhere. Start digging!"

The three men dropped to their knees. They ignored the biting cold as they began to scoop away handfuls of snow with their bare hands. The wind howled around them. It seemed to mock their efforts as it deposited fresh snow almost as quickly as they could clear it.

Emily's heart hammered against her ribs as she approached Brian's room. Her fingers trembled on the camera, the plastic felt warm and slick against her palm. She drew in a steadying breath, tasting copper on her tongue.

When she entered, Brian and Claire's heads snapped up in unison. Something dark flickered across Brian's face before he masked it with confusion. Emily forced herself to move with a calmness though every instinct screamed at her to run.

"Claire," Emily signed, her movements precise despite her trembling hands. "We need to talk."

"I have nothing to say to you." Claire's signs were sharp, cutting through the air.

Brian's eyebrows drew together in that familiar expression of concern that Emily now saw for the manipulation it was. "Everything okay?" His voice was honey-smooth, practiced.

"Yes, Brian. I just need a moment with Claire." Emily gestured to the hallway, careful to keep her face neutral.

"Well, I'm not available." Claire's words exploded from her mouth. "Whatever you have to say, you can say it right here, right now."

Emily's chest tightened. "Fine." She turned to Brian, met his eyes. "I saw the pictures. I know you orchestrated everything."

"Are you *joking*?" Claire's incredulous laugh held a note of hysteria.

"No. Look at his camera. It's full of photos of us—"

"This is a new low, Emily." Color flooded Claire's cheeks as she surged to her feet. "How *dare* you accuse him? After everything he's been through?"

Emily kept her gaze locked on Brian, searching for cracks in his facade. "I know what happened that night. I know you killed her."

The silence that followed was absolute, broken by the soft tick of the bedside clock. Brian's laugh, when it came, was just a fraction too late, too hollow. "Emily, we've been over this. Meredith killed Alice. We all know that."

Claire exploded. "For God's sake! Haven't you done enough damage? Why can't you just let this go?"

Emily's hands flew through the signs, desperate to make them understand. "Brian, the timestamp on the photo—"

"ENOUGH!" Claire's shout reverberated off the walls. "You're not just paranoid anymore, you're *insulting* the man Alice loved!"

Something in Emily snapped. Her voice, strained and unfamiliar, tore from her throat like broken glass, "He saw Alice's dead body hours before any of us woke up!"

The words seemed to hang in the air. Claire's rage crumpled into confusion, doubt seeping into her expression like poison. "What... what did you say?"

Emily's breathing came in heavily as she forced her hands to move slowly. She reached for the camera, her evidence, her weapon. "The photo of Alice's body. Timestamp: 1:14 AM. You said you didn't find her until morning."

Claire turned to Brian, her voice barely a whisper. "Brian?" The single word carried the weight of collapsing trust. "What is she talking about?"

For a moment, Brian's composure slipped. Claire took a small step back. "Brian?" she repeated.

In that instant, everything changed. Brian's hand shot out, grabbing Claire and yanking her against him. There was a metallic click, and Scott's revolver pressed firmly under Claire's chin.

Brian's grip tightened on Claire. His eyes never left Emily. A slow, unsettling smile spread across his face.

"You know, Emily," he began, his voice unnervingly calm, "I've always admired your attention to detail. The way you observe, analyze. It's ... beautiful, you know that right?"

He chuckled softly, and his smile sent chills down Emily's spine. "But you missed so much. The delicate dance of emotions, the raw humanity on display. It was exquisite."

Brian's face contorted, caught between anguish and ecstasy. "*Alice* ..." The name escaped like a prayer. "I loved her, you know. Really loved her." His hands trembled as he pressed them against his chest. 'But love—*real* love—it's the sharpest blade. When I wrapped my hands around her throat, when she realized what was happening ... God, the betrayal in her eyes. That's when I knew." His voice cracked. "You can't manufacture that kind of raw emotion. You can't stage it. You have to break something beautiful to *really* capture it." He drew a shuddering breath. "It hurt me. It hurt so much. And yet it felt ... perfect."

Claire whimpered, and Brian's attention snapped back to the present.

"Now, now, Claire." His voice was gentle, almost tender. "Your pain was exquisite. The way suspicion ate at you, corrupted your faith in everyone. That raw jealousy." He tilted his head, studying her like a precious photograph. "You gave the story so much ... depth."

His mind drifted to Emily. "And you. Your relentless hunt for truth. The way you pieced it together, never knowing you were creating exactly what I wanted."

Emily's voice cut like ice. "Because you murdered Alice. She trusted—"

"I was going to leave that night," Brian interrupted, his eyes distant. "My collection was complete with Alice. The perfect ending." His fingers twitched, as if reaching for a camera. "But then the storm ... It was like a gift. Watching you all fracture under pressure, tear at each other with doubt and fear ..." He drew in a slow breath. "It was better than anything I could have manufactured."

A strange sound escaped him, something between a laugh and a sigh. "And Meredith ... God, she was perfect. The overlooked servant, the silent witness. I could have killed her in the middle of the living room and you still wouldn't have noticed her. When I hung her up, wrote that note ..." He closed his eyes, savoring the memory. "It was like signing my masterpiece. The final brushstroke."

Brian's eyes gleamed with a manic light. "Did you look through all the photos, Emily? Did you see the beauty I created? I hope you basqued in the raw, real moments of human experience."

He pressed the gun harder against Claire's chin. "This ... this right here. This is art. This is life and death and everything in between. Don't tell me I'm seriously the only one who sees it."

Emily's hands trembled as she signed, "You're sick, Brian. This isn't art. It's psychotic."

Brian's eyes flashed dangerously. "You don't understand. You aren't seeing the beauty in it." His grip on Claire tightened, causing her to whimper. "But I can make you see. I can show you what true art looks like."

Claire's voice shook as she spoke, "Brian, please. This isn't you. We can get you help."

A bark of laughter escaped Brian's lips. "Help? I don't need help. I've never felt more alive, never more in tune with my artistic vision."

Emily took a cautious step forward, her voice steadier than her racing heart. "Let her go, Brian. It's over. They know we're here. The police are on their way." The lie tasted bitter on her tongue—for all she knew, the others were still struggling down the mountain.

Brian's smile widened. A manic glint shined in his eyes. "Even better. An audience. They can witness my greatest work yet."

Brian's eyes met Emily's, and there was something worse than madness there—a calm, absolute conviction. "I thought you of all people would understand, Emily. You're so observant, always watching, analyzing. That's what I do. I show people what they can't see about themselves."

He shifted his grasp on Claire, the gun steady against her temple. The movement was almost gentle, like adjusting a subject for a photograph. "I can show you both something beautiful. Something real."

Emily's mind raced as she watched Claire tremble in Brian's grip. She needed to distract him, to buy time, to find an opening. Constantly searching the room for anything she could use to disarm him.

Last Sunday, around 1:00 a.m.

Brian sat in the shadows of the living room, watching Alice pace near the fireplace. Everyone else had retreated to sleep, leaving them alone in the flickering firelight.

"I'm so pissed, Brian." Alice wrapped her arms around herself. "That dinner was horrible. Claire had no right to say those things. Now all of my oldest friends are looking at me like I'm some slutty mistress? What gives her the right?"

Brian's fingers caressed his camera, watching her through the viewfinder. The firelight created beautiful shadows across her face, highlighting the vulnerability in her expression.

"I just don't know," Brian's voice was eerily calm. "I saw you with David on the ski lift. The two of you were certainly comfortable. Whispering. Flirting. Apparently everyone else noticed too."

Alice turned to face him, confusion and hurt crossing her expression. "What the hell? Not you too. Nothing happened with David—we were just talking!"

"Talking!" He laughed as he set his camera down carefully. "Like how you've been 'just talking' all weekend? The secret glances, the private conversations..."

"Brian, you're starting to sound like Claire now. You're being ridiculous. If you'd just let me explain—"

"Explain what?" He rose from his chair with predatory grace. "Did David promise you something better than what I can give you?"

Alice's body shifted as she recognized the change in him—the dangerous edge to his voice. She thought about running, but knew that Brian was faster.

"Brian, okay, settle down. I don't know if we're right for each other, alright? Your temper, it's been getting worse, you know it just as well as I do."

"Shut up."

She continued, "I don't think we are compatible anymore. I won't make a scene, but when we get back to New York, I think it's time for us to go our separate ways."

"You're not about to throw away all of my hard work."

"*Your* hard work? Brian, what do you do? It's always you and your camera, and if anything is wrong you take it out on me. You need help. I don't feel comfortable being around you right now."

Brian pulled out Scott's revolver, aiming it at the center of her forehead.

Tears flowed from Alice's eyes. "Are you really going to kill me?"

Brian tossed the gun onto the floor, where it slid under the sofa. "Oh, not like this." His hands tightened around her neck. "Like this."

His grip closed with methodical precision. "Shhh," he whispered into her ear. "Just let it happen. Let me capture this moment." At 1:14 a.m., Brian watched the light fade from Alice's eyes.

With trembling hands, he reached for his camera and focused the lens on her lifeless form. The click of the shutter broke the silence. "Perfect," he breathed, reviewing the image. He looked down at Alice's body and arranged her limbs with artistic precision.

He was high with adrenaline, but instead of feeling scared, he felt stronger than ever before. He returned upstairs, knowing everyone saw him as Alice's sweet companion—eliminating him as a suspect. Pride swelled within him at the work he had begun, and excitement built for the photos he would take of the group in their inevitable suspicion of each other. This was better than any staged photograph. He was capturing these people in their most raw state.

As Brian stood poised to unleash more horror, Emily realized that she was the only thing standing between her friends and this monster who called himself an artist. The weight of that responsibility settled on her shoulders, but she knew she had to stop Brian before it was too late.

Emily searched for a way to reach Brian or distract him long enough to save Claire. She took a deep breath to steady herself.

"You're right, Brian," Emily signed confidently. "I didn't see it before. Show me. Show me your art."

Brian's expression changed with surprise but then narrowed with suspicion. "What are you playing at?"

"No games," Emily replied. Her face was a mask of forced calm. "You wanted an audience. I'm here. Show me what makes your work so special."

A slow smile spread across Brian's face. "I don't trust you. You must be stupid if you think I do."

He loosened his grip on Claire slightly. "It's all about capturing the moment. Fear. Desperation. The realization that life is slipping away."

Emily's eyes landed on Claire, whose hand was slowly inching towards a heavy crystal lamp on the nearby table.

"But it's more than just the subject," Brian continued, his voice taking on a fervent quality. "It's about the composition. The lighting. The way the fear etches itself into every line of the face. It's about capturing that perfect moment when life transitions to death, when the soul leaves the body, and all that's left is the raw, pure essence of humanity."

Emily swallowed hard against the surge of acid in her throat. The man she had considered a friend had revealed himself to be a monster. The realization made her head spin. She needed to act. Now.

"You see," Brian went on, "what I create isn't just photography. It's art in its purest form. It's life and death captured in a single frame, a testament to the fragility of human existence."

Emily made a split-second decision. With all her might, she hurled the camera to the floor. The crash echoed through the room like a gunshot, and Brian's head snapped towards the sound. His hand letting go of Claire momentarily as he reached toward the camera.

Claire seized the opportunity. Her fingers closed around the base of the lamp, and with a grunt of effort, she swung it in a wide arc. The heavy crystal connected with Brian's temple with a sickening thud. He stumbled onto the ground, momentarily stunned, wincing with shock and pain.

"Run!" Emily screamed. She grabbed Claire's arm. They bolted for the door. Every second felt like an eternity.

Behind them, they could hear Brian's roar of rage, followed by the deafening crack of gunshots. Plaster exploded from the walls around them as bullets whizzed past, missing them by mere inches. The acrid smell of gunpowder filled the air and mixed with the dust from the damaged walls.

"You bitches!" Brian's voice echoed, filled with pain and fury. "You're going to get what's coming to you. I'm going to *fucking* kill you!"

Breathlessly, Emily yanked Claire toward the master bedroom. Heavy footsteps pounded unevenly somewhere behind them.

"Help me!" Emily shouted frantically as they burst through the bedroom door. She slammed it shut, her hands trembling. "The dresser!"

They threw their weight against Claire's heavy oak dresser. The sound of wood scraping across hardwood filled the air as they pushed it in front of the door. Emily's muscles screamed with the effort, but adrenaline kept her moving.

Brian's footsteps grew closer, his voice echoing through the hallway. "You can't hide from me forever!"

Emily looked at the laundry chute's wide wooden door. The metal slide disappeared into darkness below, but she knew it led straight to the basement laundry room. A shot rang out, splintering wood near the doorframe. Emily's heart leaped into her throat.

"Go!" Emily signed, pushing Claire toward the chute. Claire wrenched open the wooden door and swung her legs into the chute, pushing off. Her figure disappeared into darkness, as she began her descent down the metal shaft.

The dresser shuddered as Brian slammed against the door. Wood cracked. Emily scrambled into the chute just as the dresser began to give way. She caught a glimpse of Brian's face in the gap between door and frame, his eyes wild with rage, before she let gravity take her.

The metal was cool against her back as she slid down into darkness. The descent seemed to last forever, the shaft twisting slightly before opening into the basement laundry room. She tumbled onto a pile of dirty clothes as Claire was already scrambling to her feet.

Above them, Brian's roar of frustration echoed down the chute, followed by the thunder of his footsteps racing for the stairs.

"The kitchen," Emily signed, pulling Claire up. "We can hide and wait for help."

They sprinted across the basement, past the storage shelves and cut rope from Meredith's demise. Their footsteps slapped against the concrete floor as they ran for the stairs, the sound of Brian's pursuit driving them forward. He was coming, and they both knew they had only seconds to find a hiding place before he caught up to them.

They burst through the kitchen door and frantically scanned the room. Emily knew they didn't want to kill Brian—they just needed to stop him long enough for Scott and the others to return. Her gaze landed on a cast-iron skillet hanging from a rack. She grabbed it, the weight reassuring in her hands. If they could just knock him out ... Beside her, Claire had armed herself with a fire extinguisher from the corner.

"Behind the island," Emily whispered. They ducked behind the large kitchen island and tried to muffle their panicked breathing.

The kitchen now felt like a corner they had backed into. Every shadow seemed to move, the old lodge groaning around them like a living thing. The tick of the clock on the wall marked each passing second, each moment bringing Brian closer to discovering their hiding place.

Emily and Claire exchanged a look of compassion. They both knew that this game of cat and mouse couldn't last forever. Sooner or later, they would have to face Brian. And when that moment came, they would be ready.

The floorboards in the hallway vibrated with approaching steps, the pounding echoing off the tiles. Emily tightened her grip on the skillet, her palms slick with sweat. Beside her, Claire had already pulled the pin from the fire extinguisher, holding the nozzle ready.

"Emily? Claire?" Brian's voice drifted through the door, unnervingly calm after his earlier outburst. "Come now, don't make this harder than it needs to be. We were creating something beautiful together. Can't you see that?"

Emily held her breath, waiting for the inevitable fight. She could see Claire's chest rising and falling rapidly. The kitchen door inched open with a low groan. Brian's shadow stretched across the floor, growing larger as he stalked toward their hiding place.

"I know you're in here," Brian sang. "I can feel you. The fear. The anticipation ... It's exquisite. This is the climax we've been building towards, the perfect finale to our story."

He moved around the kitchen, opening cabinets and drawers. Each sound made Claire flinch, certain that at any moment he would discover their hiding place.

"You know," Brian continued, vibrations from his voice growing closer, "I always thought you'd be the one to figure it out, Emily. You're so smart. It's one of the things I admire about you. But you just couldn't leave well enough alone, could you?"

Emily's mind raced, trying to formulate a plan. They couldn't stay hidden forever, but facing Brian head-on seemed too risky. Unfortunately, that was their only option. She looked at Claire, and she saw her own fear and desperation mirrored in her friend's eyes.

Suddenly, Brian's voice came from directly above them. "Found you."

Emily's heart stopped. She looked up to see Brian's face. A cruel smile twisted his face as he peered over the edge of the island at them. For a second, time seemed to stand still as they stared at each other—the hunter and the hunted locked in a moment of terrible recognition.

While Brian leered down at them, Emily and Claire sprang into action. Claire unleashed a cloud of white foam directly into Brian's face. He staggered back, coughing and blinded by the chemical spray.

Emily swung the cast-iron skillet into Brian's leg with a sickening crunch. Howling in pain, he fired one shot at the ceiling before collapsing to the floor.

"Come on!" Emily shouted and grabbed Claire's hand. They bolted from behind the island and toward the kitchen door.

But Brian, despite his injuries, wasn't done. He lunged forward, managing to grab Claire's ankle. She fell hard and cried out as she hit the floor.

Emily turned back. She raised the skillet again, but Brian was quicker. He pointed the gun at Claire's head, his eyes wild with rage and pain.

"Don't move," he snarled. His breath came in ragged gasps. "This ends now."

Emily froze. They were so close to escape, but now they were right back where they started—at Brian's mercy.

His finger moved on the trigger. Then, the kitchen door burst open. Mark stood at the entrance, his face a mask of determination and rage.

Mark launched himself at Brian. The two men collided. The gun fired with a deafening bang. The bullet embedded itself in the cupboards while they grappled on the floor.

Emily rushed to Claire's side, helped her up, and pulled her away from the fight. They watched in horror as Mark and Brian struggled, each fighting for control of the gun.

Brian fought with the desperation of a cornered animal. He managed to slam the back of the gun into Mark's forehead, dazing him momentarily.

The gun trembled in Brian's grasp, but Mark lunged with desperate precision. His fingers clamped around Brian's wrist as he drove his elbow down, smashing Brian's forearm against the cold tile. The impact rang through Mark's bones, but Brian's finger still found the trigger.

Thunder cracked in the confined space. White-hot pain blazed across Mark's bicep as the bullet carved a path through flesh. Blood spattered Brian's shirt, dark drops spreading like ink on fabric. The metallic scent of it filled Mark's nostrils, mixing with gunpowder and sweat.

Mark channeled the pain into raw strength, twisting Brian's wrist at an impossible angle until tendons and muscle gave way. The revolver skittered across the floor, spinning away into shadow. In the same motion, Mark slammed his weight down, using his knees to pin Brian's shoulders. His breath came in ragged bursts.

"It's over," Mark growled through clenched teeth, tasting blood. Sweat dripped from his chin onto Brian's face below. "Give. Up."

Brian bucked and thrashed, but Mark bore down harder, feeling the fight drain from his opponent like air from a punctured tire. Brian's struggles weakened to tremors, then stillness.

The kitchen door burst inward with a bang that made them both flinch. Scott and David stood frozen in the doorway, their faces masks of shock as they took in the tableau of violence before them: blood on tile, overturned chairs, and two men locked in the aftermath of desperate combat.

"The police are on their way," Scott announced, moving quickly to help Mark secure Brian. "We managed to get through to them at a gas station down the mountain."

As Scott used his belt to bind Brian's hands and feet, Emily felt an abundance of relief wash over her. It was over. They had survived.

She looked at Mark who was now standing and holding his bleeding arm. Their eyes met, and in that moment, a silent understanding passed between them. The past was the past. Mark had proven himself when it mattered most.

"Thank you," Emily signed, her hands shaking slightly.

Mark nodded, a small smile tugging at his lips. "Always," he replied simply.

Emily slowly started to feel some of the tension of the past few days begin to dissipate. There would be questions to answer, statements to give, and trauma to process. But for now, at this moment, they were safe. They had survived the nightmare of Belmont Lodge, and they had done it together.

The group huddled close, offering comfort and support to one another as they waited for the authorities to arrive. Brian, subdued and bound, lay on his stomach in the corner under Scott's watchful eye.

CHAPTER THIRTEEN—Aftermath

The wail of sirens pierced the frigid mountain air as a convoy of police vehicles, ambulances, and fire trucks wound their way up the snow-covered road to Belmont Lodge. The storm had finally abated. At the bottom of the mountain, an excavator carved through the deep snow, forging a path for the line of emergency vehicles that followed.

As they approached the lodge, the full extent of the group's isolation became clear. Snow had entombed the building, pressing against windows and doors, the weight of it threatening to crush inward.

Inside the lodge, Emily, Claire, Scott, Mark, and David huddled together in the living room, their eyes fixed on the bound and sullen form of Brian. The adrenaline that had fueled their fight for survival was beginning to ebb, replaced by bone-deep exhaustion and the first tendrils of shock.

The sound of the excavator's engine grew louder, accompanied by shouted orders and the crunch of boots on snow. Suddenly, there was a tremendous crash as the front doors were broken down by a team of firefighters.

"Police! Everyone stay where you are!"

Scott, his police instincts kicking in despite his fatigue, stepped forward with his hands raised. "I'm a police officer—Officer Scott Simmons, Glenwood Utah, Badge 247," he called out, his voice hoarse. "The situation is under control. The suspect is restrained."

The lead officer, a stern-faced woman with graying hair, gestured to her team. They moved swiftly to secure Brian, who offered no resistance as he was handcuffed and read his rights.

While Brian was led away, Emily couldn't help but shudder at the vacant look in his eyes. The man who had been their friend, who had shared meals and laughter with them just days ago, was now a stranger—a monster wearing a familiar face.

Paramedics streamed in behind the police, immediately moving to check on the group. Emily watched numbly as they examined Claire's bruises, cleaned the cuts on Mark's knuckles, and checked David for signs of hypothermia. The flurry of activity around her felt surreal as if she were watching it all happen from a great distance.

The lead officer approached Scott, her expression grave. "Officer Simmons, I'm Detective Shaw. What happened here?"

Scott nodded. "Brian Hansen confessed to the murders of Alice Thompson and Meredith Nowak." He paused and took a deep breath. "The victims' bodies are in the basement freezer. We ... We had to move them."

Detective Shaw's posture altered slightly, but she quickly regained her composure. "Thank you, Officer Simmons. We'll take it from here." She turned to her team and issued rapid-fire orders to secure the basement and process the scene.

As the police and forensics team descended to the basement, Emily felt a rush of nausea wash over her. The clinical terms they used—"victims," "bodies," and "scene"—seemed to strip away Alice and Meredith's humanity.

A gentle touch on her arm made Emily flinch. She looked up to see a young paramedic, who made sure to face her directly as he spoke. "Are you injured anywhere?" he asked, kind and carefully so she could read his lips.

Emily shook her head. Cuts and bruises meant nothing at this point. She just wanted to go home.

The paramedic moved on, satisfied that she needed no immediate medical attention. Emily's eyes moved back to Scott. He still spoke with Detective Shaw. His posture was rigid and his face set in the cold air. But Emily could see the slight tremor in his hands, the tightness around his eyes.

Detective Shaw finally turned back to the group, her face solemn. "I know you've all been through a terrible ordeal. While we can conduct questioning here, you might be more comfortable giving your statements at the station, away from...We can handle this however you prefer."

Emily nodded, feeling a strange sense of relief at the suggestion. Yes, there would be questions to answer and a story to tell, but somewhere else—anywhere else than this lodge with its dark corners and haunted memories.

As they were led out to the waiting police cars, Emily cast a glance back at the lodge. In the glare of the floodlights, it looked almost alien. Its snow-covered roof and broken door were testaments to the horrors it had witnessed. She knew the truth that lay behind its once-picturesque facade and the secrets it now held.

With a shudder, she turned away and allowed herself to be guided into a waiting car. When the door closed behind her, Emily felt as if a chapter of her life was ending. However, she was brushed with glimmering hope, and the promise that the future would be brighter than the past.

When they finally arrived, the police station was a hive of activity. Officers bustled about, phones rang incessantly, and the air buzzed with an energy that felt at odds with Emily's exhaustion. They were ushered into a large room with fluorescent lights that were harsh after days of firelight and shadows.

"Wait here," Detective Shaw instructed. "We'll take your statements individually. Try to rest if you can, grab some coffee. This may take a while."

As the detective left, Emily sank into a hard plastic chair where her body felt every bruise, every ache. She looked around at her friends and saw weariness reflected in their faces.

Mark paced restlessly. David slumped in the corner. Claire sat with her arms wrapped tightly around herself, her mind distant.

"Hey," David called out to Claire, "Do you want some coffee?"

Claire sniffled a bit, "No I'm okay."

"It's really no problem," David tried, "I was going to get some for myself."

"I said I'm okay, David." It was clear that even the resolve of everything the group had endured, would not be enough to reconcile their marriage.

Scott moved to sit beside Emily. "How are you holding up?" he asked softly.

Emily's hands moved to sign but faltered. How could she put her maelstrom of emotions into words? Instead, she simply leaned against Scott's shoulder and drew comfort from his solid presence.

Time seemed to lose all meaning as they waited. Emily drifted in and out of a light doze. She jerked awake at every sudden sound, her heart racing before reality reasserted itself. She was safe now. Brian was under police custody. It was over.

And yet, as Emily watched a pair of officers lead a handcuffed Brian past their room, she couldn't shake the feeling that it could never truly be over. The haunted look in Brian's eyes, the small smile that played at the edges of his mouth—it all served to remind her that the monster they had discovered was very real and had been hiding in plain sight all along.

After what felt like hours, Detective Shaw returned with a woman Emily hadn't seen before. "Emily," The woman signed, "We're ready for you now. My name is Sandra Redd, I'm an ASL interpreter for the police department, I figured you would feel more comfortable communicating through ASL especially at a time like this."

Emily smiled, "Yes, that sounds perfect."

With a deep breath, Emily stood. Her legs felt weak, her body protesting the hours spent in the hard plastic chair. Scott gave her hand a reassuring squeeze as she passed, and she managed a weak smile in return.

Following Detective Shaw and Sandra down a narrow hallway, Emily found herself in what appeared to be the detective's office. A wooden desk occupied one side while a pair of leather armchairs sat before it, more comfortable than Emily had expected. Sandra positioned herself beside Detective Shaw's desk where Emily could easily see both women.

"Please, have a seat," Sandra signed, interpreting Detective Shaw's words. As Emily sat down, the detective placed a voice recorder on the table. "Do you mind if I record our conversation? It'll help us keep an accurate record."

Emily nodded, relieved she could communicate in ASL. Her hands had been itching to sign; speaking aloud felt especially difficult after the trauma of the past few days.

Detective Shaw pressed a button on the recorder. Through Sandra's interpretation, she said, "This is Detective Karen Shaw, interviewing Emily Parker regarding the incidents at Belmont Lodge. Emily, can you please say and spell your full name and date of birth for the record?"

Emily signed her response, "My name is Emily Parker, E-M-I-L-Y P-A-R-K-E-R, I was born November 4th 1996." Sandra's clear voice speaking for the record.

"Thank you," Sandra signed, interpreting the detective's words. "Now, Emily, I know this is difficult, but I need you to walk me through everything that happened, from the beginning. Take your time, and don't leave anything out, no matter how insignificant it might seem."

Emily took a deep breath, gathering her thoughts. Where to begin? The excited packing for what should have been a fun reunion? The first uneasy feelings as they arrived at the lodge? The moment she realized something was wrong?

Her hands moved with growing confidence as she signed, Sandra's voice carrying her story. "The lodge was beautiful, but there was something ... off about it. I couldn't put my finger on it at first."

As Emily recounted the events, Detective Shaw listened intently, occasionally jotting down notes or asking questions through Sandra. Emily's signs became more emphatic as she described the growing tension among the friends, the strange occurrences, and the horrifying discovery of Alice's body. Her hands trembled slightly when she recalled finding Meredith, the word "GUILTY" a mocking suicide note.

"And that's when you began to suspect Brian?" came the detective's question through Sandra's interpretation.

Emily's signs were controlled and certain now. "Not at first. We all thought ... We all thought Meredith had killed Alice and then herself out of guilt. But things didn't add up. And then I found the camera."

She explained the timestamp on the photo of Alice's body, her signing growing more intense as she detailed the evidence that had led to her confrontation with Brian. When she reached the part about Brian's confession and subsequent attack, her hands moved rapidly, as if trying to get through the terrifying memory as quickly as possible.

"He was ... he was so calm about it," Emily signed, her movements becoming smaller, more controlled. "He talked about murder like it was paint. Like what he'd done to Alice, to Meredith, was something beautiful."

"Can you walk me through exactly how you and Claire managed to escape?" Sandra interpreted Detective Shaw's careful questioning.

Emily nodded, her hands telling the story of their frantic flight through the lodge, the desperate fight in the kitchen, and finally, Mark's timely intervention. When she finished, she felt drained, as if she'd relived every moment of terror and uncertainty.

"Thank you, Emily," Detective Shaw said, her voice gentle. "I know that wasn't easy."

The detective stood up, "You've been very helpful, Emily. There are victim support services available if you need them."

As Emily stood to leave, she felt a weight lift from her shoulders. She had told her story, and had given voice to the horrors they'd experienced. It wasn't over. She knew there would be more questions, more statements, and a trial eventually. But for now, she had done what she could to ensure that Alice and Meredith would get justice.

Stepping out of the interrogation room, Emily felt as if she were emerging from a long, dark tunnel. The fluorescent lights of the police station seemed brighter somehow. The bustling activity around her was a reminder that life went on even in the face of unimaginable tragedy.

As she made her way back to her friends, Emily allowed herself to hope, just a little, that the worst was behind them.

One by one, the others were called in for questioning. Claire went next. Mark paced until it was his turn while David sat in stoic silence. Scott was the last to be interviewed, his law enforcement background likely prompting a more detailed questioning.

Emily continued to catch herself falling asleep. The fluorescent lights, the office full of people, and the occasional swimming around in a small fish tank all blended into a surreal backdrop. She startled every time the door opened, half-expecting to see Brian's face, that eerie calm still etched on his face.

Hours passed. Other officers came and went, some casting curious glances at the group. A kind-faced woman who introduced herself as a victim advocate brought them coffee and sandwiches, but Emily could barely stomach more than a few bites. The food tasted like ash in her mouth, and her body was still too stressed to process hunger normally.

Finally, as the first hints of dawn began to color the sky outside, Detective Shaw reappeared. She looked as tired as they felt, dark circles under her eyes testament to the long night.

"We've processed your statements," she began. "There will be more questions in the days to come, but for now, you're free to go home. We'll be in touch regarding the ongoing investigation and any necessary court proceedings."

She paused, and her expression softened slightly. "I want you all to know that there are services available to you, should you need them. What you've been through ... It's not something anyone should have to experience. It's a good thing you have one another. Please don't hesitate to reach out if you need help."

Emily barely registered the business card the detective pressed into her hand. The idea of going home felt almost as surreal as the events of the past few days. How could they simply walk out of here and return to their normal lives?

As if reading her thoughts, Mark spoke up. "What about the lodge? And ... and the bodies?"

Detective Shaw's face grew strict. "The lodge is now an active crime scene. Our forensics team will be there for several days, maybe weeks. As for Ms. Thompson and Ms. Nowak, their bodies will be transported to the county morgue for full autopsies. We'll release them to the families as soon as we can."

The clinical way she spoke of Alice and Meredith sent a chill down Emily's spine.

"And Brian?" Claire asked, her voice beginning to crack.

"Mr. Hansen is in custody," Detective Shaw replied. "He'll be arraigned later today. Given the severity of the charges and the evidence against him, I don't anticipate he'll be granted bail."

A collective sigh of relief passed through the group. The idea of Brian walking free, even temporarily, was too horrifying to contemplate.

"Now," the detective continued, "I've arranged for transportation to take you all to your vehicles. Unless there's anything else ...?"

They shook their heads, too exhausted to form coherent questions. As the squad car drove them back to the lodge, Emily found herself staring out the car window. She knew she had done everything she needed to do. Now it was over.

The outside world was awash in the gray light of early morning. Emily gravitated towards Scott. She didn't want to be separated from him ever again.

When they got out of the car, in the driveway, Scott stopped short at the sight before him. There was the shop owner—the man he'd dismissed as nothing more than a nosey local—quietly clearing snow from their vehicles in the driveway. His good eye was focused on his work, his breaths creating small clouds in the cold air as he methodically pushed the snow away with an old wooden-handled shovel. Scott felt a pang of shame for his earlier judgment. Here was kindness, asked for by no one, witnessed by accident. Through the falling snow, Scott's gaze fixed on his own truck, its familiar outline somehow comforting, a last tangible link to their life before the nightmare began.

"Thank you," Scott called over to the man.

The man lifted his head looking at Scott, "Figured you went through an awful lot the past few days. Least I could do is help."

As they prepared to leave, Emily caught sight of Claire and David. The exhausted couple stood close together. They exchanged only a silent nod of understanding. They had endured hell together, and that shared experience bound them in a way that defied explanation.

Mark stood a little apart from the others, his posture tense and his eyes haunted. Emily approached him. Without a word, she wrapped her arms around him.

Mark returned the hug, and his body shook slightly. Her sight remained on Scott's truck, still parked where they'd left it days ago. Emily felt the weight of everything they'd experienced settle over her. Scott opened her door, offering his hand to help her out. She climbed inside as he walked around the front of the truck and into his seat.

Emily turned to face Scott. "I don't want to be alone anymore."

Scott's eyes softened. "You don't have to be," he signed back. "Not ever again."

He gently lifted her chin, his touch feather-light, and pressed a soft kiss on her lips. No words—signed or spoken—were necessary. They had survived the darkness together, and whatever came next, they would face it the same way.

Scott cranked the cold engine and waited a moment before starting the road trip home. They were going back to their normal lives, but nothing felt normal anymore.

The familiar road to Glenwood stretched out before them, but Emily found no comfort in the sight. Six hours on the road to reflect on everything that had just unfolded.

They had barely been on the road for a few minutes when Emily felt something inside her break. A sob tore from her throat. She buried her face in her hands, and her body shook with the force of her cries.

Wordlessly, Scott placed his hand on her back. He simply let her cry, understanding that this release was necessary, that she finally felt safe enough to let the tears fall—tears of grief for Alice, tears of relief for their survival, tears of gratitude for finding love amid horror.

As they drove away from the mountain, leaving the lodge and its mysteries behind, Emily reached for Scott's hand. Their fingers intertwined, a silent promise of all that lay ahead.

While Emily's sobs echoed in the confines of the truck, the road stretched on before them, leading them back to a world that would never quite look the same again.

EPILOGUE

Glenwood, Utah – 3 years later

The warm glow of the "6" and "0" candles illuminated Michael's face as Emily and Scott finished singing. His eyes crinkled at the corners as he surveyed the small gathering - just his daughter and son-in-law, exactly how he wanted it.

"Make a wish, Dad," Emily signed, the delicate diamond on her ring finger catching the candlelight.

Michael closed his eyes for a moment, then blew out the candles in one determined breath. Emily clapped while Scott snapped a photo.

"Time for presents!" Scott announced, placing a carefully wrapped package in front of his father-in-law.

Michael raised an eyebrow. "You two didn't have to get me anything. Having you here is more than enough."

But Emily was already pushing the gift closer, practically bouncing with anticipation. Michael carefully peeled back the wrapping paper to reveal a familiar brown box. His breath caught as he ran his fingers over the Clue logo.

"Oh, Emmy," he whispered, a single tear rolling down his cheek. The memory hit him with startling clarity - Emily at five years old, cross-legged on the living room floor in her favorite star-patterned pajamas, studying the game board with fierce concentration. Those quiet evenings spent together, just the two of them, moving pieces around the mansion and solving mysteries.

Emily squeezed his hand. "Remember how you used to let me win?" she signed with a knowing smile.

"Let you win?" Michael let out a warm laugh. "I couldn't beat you!"

Scott's phone buzzed. After checking the screen, he excused himself to take the call, stepping onto the back porch.

"One more gift," Emily signed, pulling out a smaller box.

"Emmy, really, I don't need-"

But she was already placing it in his hands. Michael opened it, then froze. Inside was a small white onesie with "World's Best Grandpa" printed across the front.

His hands trembled as he lifted it out of the box. "Is this... are you...?"

Emily nodded, pulling an ultrasound photo from her purse. Her father's eyes welled with tears as he studied the grainy image.

"We just found out it's a girl," Emily signed, her own eyes glistening. "I wanted to wait to tell you today."

Michael pulled his daughter into a tight embrace. When they finally separated, he asked, "Do you have a name picked out?"

"Alice," Emily signed. Her father's expression softened with understanding.

"After your friend?" he asked gently. "The one who-"

Emily nodded, wiping her eyes. Before she could respond, Scott returned, looking apologetic.

"I'm so sorry," he said, "but I got a call-" He stopped, noticing Michael's tears and the scene before him. "Wait. Did you tell him?"

Emily gave a sheepish smile. "Yes! Sorry, I couldn't wait another minute."

Scott's surprised expression melted into a warm grin. "Well, I guess the cat's out of the bag." He moved to hug his father-in-law. "We're having a baby, Mike."

As Emily began to cut the birthday cake, Scott continued, "I'm so sorry to cut this short, but they need me at the station."

"Go," Emily signed. "Dad and I have some mysteries to solve anyway." She gestured to the Clue board with a smile.

After Scott left, Emily and her father settled in with the game board between them, just like old times. The familiar ritual of moving pieces, gathering clues, and making careful deductions felt like coming home.

Later that evening, Emily busied herself in the kitchen of their cozy Glenwood home. The sound of sizzling vegetables filled the air. Scott came up behind her, wrapping his arms around her waist, placing a gentle hand on her barely visible bump.

"Mark just texted," he said. "He and Isabella are on their way. Freshly engaged, we have to remember to bring out the champagne."

Emily smiled, leaning back into his embrace. "I've missed them," she signed. "It's been too long."

As if on cue, the doorbell rang. Scott went to answer it, and soon the house was filled with the warm greetings of old friends. Mark's face was more relaxed than Emily had ever seen him. Isabella, a tall woman with kind eyes, greeted Emily with a tight hug.

They settled around the dining table, and conversation flowed easily as they caught up on each other's lives. Scott raised his glass of champagne. "Congratulations again on the engagement, you two. Really happy for you both." He exchanged a knowing look with Emily. "Actually, we have some news of our own..."

Mark's eyes darted between them, then landed on Emily's water glass. His face lit up with realization. "You're serious!? Pregnant?" He jumped up from his seat, breaking into a wide grin. "I'm so happy for you guys!" He moved around the table, wrapping each of them in a big hug. "Em, you've been drinking water all night - I should have known!"

The years since Belmont Lodge had changed Mark in ways Emily never expected. He'd moved back to Glenwood, started therapy, and slowly rebuilt his relationships. Where there had once been anger and defensiveness, there was now openness and genuine warmth. He'd met Isabella at a local coffee shop two years ago, and Emily had watched him gradually become the person he'd always had the potential to be. Sometimes it felt surreal to remember the Mark from high school – now he was one of their closest friends, someone they had dinner with almost weekly, someone they could trust completely.

Later that night, after Mark and Isabella had left, Emily sat at the foot of her bed, one hand resting on her abdomen while her mind wandered back to the Belmont Lodge. So many questions remained unanswered, so many inexplicable events still nagged at the edges of her memory.

As she lay down, she looked over to her bookshelf where Lily's diary sat. Its worn leather cover was now as familiar as an old friend. She'd read it countless times over the years, trying to understand the connection between Lily's experiences and their own. The diary had become a talisman of sorts.

The mysterious entries, the disappearances, the supernatural theories about the lodge, was any of it true? Emily had decided at that moment that for her, it wasn't. Nobody exists purely in darkness or light. We are all responsible for our own actions and choices. Brian had given in to his despicable cravings and committed the most heinous evil. Alice, she had lived choosing goodness and love, until the very end.

Emily believed there was nothing supernatural in this world. If something didn't make sense, it simply meant she hadn't solved the puzzle yet.

A Message from the Author

Thank you to the half-dozen individuals who read this book before publication and helped with editing. Any remaining mistakes are entirely my own.

I fell in love with this story while writing it. Growing up with a deaf sister, I had the privilege of learning about deaf culture through her experiences and perspective. While I am not deaf myself, this story—Emily's story—is about a witty individual who notices details others seem to pass by. When imagining someone so perceptive and less distracted by the noise that occupies her friends, my mind naturally gravitated toward making her deaf. The heightened awareness I've witnessed in deaf individuals made Emily's role as a sleuth feel like a natural fit for her character.

The same could be said for Emily being a woman. Both aspects of her character emerged naturally as I wrote.

I've always loved telling stories, whether I'm writing songs, crafting poems, or spinning tales like this one. Language is the most fascinating thing about humans, and how we always find ways to communicate. It's a bridge we build from us to others and that is something beautiful. While writing this, I wasn't trying to appeal to every demographic or reach the masses. Instead, I had a simpler motivation: to tell my sister a really good story.

Thank you for reading.

- K